CENTER STREET

ALSO BY LEONARD WISE

The Big Biazarro

The Diggstown Ringer (Diggstown)

Dumachas and Sheba (Dumachas)

Doc's Legacy

Center Street

CENTER STREET

LEONARD WISE

BASTION PRESS

Cover and interior design by Myaypriya Long, Bookwrights Design
www.bookwrights.com
Text set in Berkeley Oldstyle, Woodtype Two, and Hopper scetches
Printed in the United States of America

Publisher's Cataloging-in-Publication
(Provided by Quality Books, Inc.)

Wise, Leonard.
    Center Street: a novel/by Leonard Wise. —
1st ed.
        p. cm.
        LCCN: 00-103370
        ISBN: 0-9700872-1-7

    1. Hudson (N.Y.)—Fiction.   2. Hudson River
Valley (N.Y. and N.J.)—Fiction.   3. Organized
crime—Fiction.   I. Title.

PS3573.I79C46 2000   813.6
                    QBI00-505

BASTION PRESS

Bastion Press
10573 West Pico Blvd., #8
Los Angeles, CA 90064

10 9 8 7 6 5 4 3 2 1

Dedicated To:

All of the children of Hudson, New York,
and the ones I grew up with, including
and especially my High School class mates,
who more than inspired this story.

Based on a True incident

However, this book is predominately fable and all of the characters are fictitious. Any resemblance to persons, living or dead, is purely coincidental.

CENTER STREET

1

When Joseph Sherman put out the word that he was interested in the incident, he received a few leads. Some of the information was suspect, and much of it obviously fabricated. Learning little in Manhattan, he decided to drive a hundred miles north on the Taconic State Parkway to the city of Hudson. Based on the information he had acquired, he was surprised by what he found: a pleasant, middle and working-class river town with two-story wooden houses, a few small industries, scenic parks, and an abundance of art, culture and small town sophistication. It appeared old and safe like many other cities with a population of less than nine thousand. The main street with its dozens of quaint antique shops, restored buildings and lampposts, and a train station reconstructed to its earliest design, was contrary to what Joseph expected. Not only that, the people were warm, friendly and helpful. The first hint of the city's tragic past came when an alcoholic vagrant boasted that he was once a "Warrior." Then, before passing out, he asked for money to buy a drink.

Joseph was actually making friends and was welcomed like any other tourist until he started asking some particularly touchy questions. His new friends were suddenly busy, and a tall, handsome, brunette lady wearing a fur-lined trench coat, began tailing him. She would stand on the opposite side of the street, or remain in a nearby car. When he attempted to speak to her, she ignored him.

Plus, the telephone in his motel room woke him a few times during the night. When Joseph complained the next morning, the desk clerk swore it was impossible because the switchboard was shut down from midnight until 6 a.m.

"You're full of crap," Joseph said.

The clerk, a pockmarked, stocky, sallow-faced young man, took offence at Joseph's remark. After glaring at him, he grinned and said, "It ain't me runnin' around some town where I ain't wanted."

"Are you sure about that?" Joseph asked.

"You cruisin' for a bruisin'?"

"What if I am?"

"Because if I wouldn't lose my job," the clerk replied, "I'd come across this desk and wipe the floor up with you."

"You call this a job?"

The two of them stared at each other, and then Joseph said, "Well?"

"If I was you, I'd haul ass on back down to New York City where it's safe."

Joseph chuckled and said, "I guess that means you want to keep the job and your teeth."

After waiting for a reply, Joseph shrugged and went outside.

The air was frigid and there were patches of snow on the streets, nonetheless Joseph chose to walk around town. He became aware that he was now being watched wherever he went. At the River Diner, on 7th Street, he took a seat at the counter and waited for more than five minutes before one of the three waitresses finally delivered a cup of coffee and took his order. As other customers arrived, they made it a point to sit away from him.

Later that morning he went to the Columbus County Library on North Fourth Street. It was a gray, stone structure dating from the early 1930s. When Joseph entered, he was surprised there wasn't a large room with the usual lines of tables. Instead, he found a cramped hallway that led off into several small rooms stocked with hardcover books, and a narrow, rickety staircase leading to the second floor.

Joseph stood just inside the front door. The building was quiet, appeared empty and smelled of musty old books, old rooms, or old women. He heard someone whispering. He thought they said, "He's here." But he wasn't certain. To the left was an office barely large enough to accommodate its wooden desk. A woman of fifty or so, chunky, sunny-faced and neatly dressed, came and sat at the desk. Aware Joseph was standing there, she feigned surprise when she looked up. "Oh, may I help you, sir?"

"Yes, you can. I'm doing some research on this area and I was wondering if you had any of the local newspapers from the late fifties?"

"Oh, I'm sure we do," she boasted proudly. "What year exactly were you interested in?"

Joseph said the summer of 1959 and waited for a reaction. The woman didn't flinch. "I believe we just happen to be out of that period right now."

"Now how did I know you were going to say that?"

"Perhaps I can help you." Another woman was standing out in the hallway. Dressed in a gray suit, she appeared to be in her late forties with a demeanor of authority.

"I'm sure you can help me, but will you?" Joseph said.

"If you're looking for clippings for the summer of fifty-nine, I'm afraid those were mislaid. If you will be so kind as to leave your name and number, we will contact you the second they're recovered."

"Will you also contact me when the dinosaurs return?"

"I beg your pardon?"

"Let me see the papers, lady. I'm not here to hurt anybody."

"Perhaps you didn't understand me."

"Oh, I understand. I'm just wondering why."

"Is there anything else we can help you with?"

"If I thought you would, I'd certainly make another request. Tell me, are you all part of the same conspiracy?"

"Conspiracy? I have no idea what you're talking about."

"The hell you don't."

As Joseph turned to walk outside, the woman said, "Have a pleasant day, Mr. Sherman."

Annoyed and frustrated, Joseph decided to return to Manhattan.

December passed into mid-January and the city appeared frozen. Its skyscrapers stood rigid, erect, as if they were icy stalagmites that took decades to push up through the asphalt sidewalks. The sky, corrugated and gray, held a large ball of faint rouge deep in the eastern rise. The sun's chances of burning through the indomitable wall of clouds were nil, because the northeast was in the fiercest, darkest days of winter. For several days the city was caught in the throes of such a bitter duration that breathing was difficult, walking strenuous, and the sun provided little or no relief.

Rushing from the Pierre Hotel, west on 61st Street and out across Fifth Avenue, his mop of brown hair bobbed in the wind. Of slender, medium build, yet solid, Joseph Sherman, 29, was never more anxious as he stood frowning and cursing at each occupied taxicab.

After a year of frustration, Joseph debated whether to give up the chase. He was close to admitting defeat when his interest was piqued again at an upper East Side holiday party. A pleasant gentleman was telling a humorous yarn about getting lost in the boondocks of upstate New York. When he mentioned the city of Hudson, Joseph anxiously waited to get the man alone. He finally did, but when he expressed interest, the gentleman simply patted his cheek and said, "You don't want to know about that."

"But I honestly do."

The man smiled, shook his head and, as he walked away, said, "No, you don't. You just think you do."

After the party Joseph attempted once again to put the story aside. However, enticing bits of information kept cropping up. He was a sports "Quips and Quotes" writer for the Herald. As someone put it, "In the department store of life, sports belongs in the toy section."

Now he was close to the story. There was a direct connection to the "Strategist," a man who had agreed to an interview that very afternoon. Joseph needed permission from his boss, Wendall Henry, the editor-in-chief of the Herald, who had already firmly rejected the idea. Wendall argued that Joseph was chasing a fairy tale, playing detective, or hard-boiled reporter, thus wasting time instead of doing his job. And with all of this, Wendall was having a farewell breakfast with friends before going on a three-week vacation with his wife through the vanishing Amazon Rain Forest.

The breakfast was from nine to ten. Wendall would join Mrs. Henry at United Airlines at 11 o'clock. Joseph checked his watch: 9:52. "Oh, God." His prayers were answered when a cab pulled up to the curb.

"The Buoy Club, 43rd and Lex."

"I know where it is," the cabby shot back.

Closing his eyes, Joseph began to compose his plea. Running the words over in his mind, he feared they wouldn't work. He decided to change his tactics, but first he took a peek at how far they had progressed: Fifth Avenue and 51st Street.

"Let me do just this one interview," Joseph mumbled to himself. "You'll read it and if you still think it's worthless, I'll never bring it up again."

The cabby slammed on his brakes, throwing Joseph against the front seat.

"Goddamn bicycle messengers!" the driver yelled. "I clipped one last week, sent his ass to Bellevue. Hope the son-of-a-bitch dies."

The driver had actually stopped the cab to make this pronouncement. Joseph wanted to beg him to keep moving, but feared a tirade that would freeze them at Fifth Avenue and 48th Street.

Finally moving again, Joseph sighed in relief and closed his eyes to rehearse. "I know you think it's a waste of time, but it has become increasingly obvious that something happened in Hudson. And why is everyone trying to keep it a secret? You can fire me, sir, if this doesn't bear out to something. Please, let me do the interview and-"

"We're here, kid. Open yer eyes."

Joseph looked up in disbelief. He handed the cabby a ten-dollar bill without noticing the price on the meter before rushing from the car.

Exuding confidence and efficiency, Wendall T.S. Henry, a silverhaired man in a Brooks Brothers suit and top coat, stood with three friends on the stone steps of the century-old Buoy Club. Assuming it was unwise to intrude, Joseph remained at the curb. The men were laughing, then shook hands with Wendall as they walked away. When he turned and saw Joseph, Wendall said, "I don't care what it is, I'm not going back to that office. Tell Beckman to handle it."

"It's not the office, sir."

"Oh, Joseph, for God's sake, not Hudson again."

"I have an interview with one of the original members. He's at the Pierre Hotel and he has-"

"No!" Wendall shouted. "If you don't want to work in sports and sports alone, quit the paper. It was your idea. You're bright enough to have your choice, but chose sports. Now, either do your job or go freelance. I have a plane to catch."

"I can't believe they even have you scared."

"I'm not scared!" Wendall shouted. "It's a dead issue. You better listen to me, Joseph. If I come back from vacation and learn that

7

you've been chasing this pipe dream...you're fired."

Staring at Joseph, Wendall took an uneasy breath and lowered his voice. "You're a good writer, son. An excellent reporter. You have a future in this business." Wendall looked around before continuing. "I was raised upstate. My wife and I still take weekends up there. Just between you and me, I know about Hudson."

"Then why don't you tell me what you know and save me some time?"

After an exasperated pause, Wendall asked. "What is it with you? What the hell are you after?"

"The story."

"There is no goddamned story! Tell me, what are you after, Joseph?" Staring at him, Wendall said, "It's not the story, is it, son?" When Joseph didn't reply, Wendall said, "You really don't want to get mixed up in that. There is no story there for you."

"But there is, and you know it."

"I'm telling you, I'm warning you, I am ordering you to let it go. Why don't you concentrate on the Super Bowl? It promises to be a great one this year. Write a good story and I'll see you get a front-page column." Wendall looked around again. "Joseph, nothing and no one worth a damn has ever come out of that town. It all ended long ago, so forget about it."

"I can't forget it."

"Then you know the consequences."

Wendall hailed a cab.

After watching the chief disappear, Joseph lowered his head and walked west on 43rd Street. Coming to a phone booth he stopped. Moments went by as he debated with himself. He felt he was much too close now to let it go.

Depositing a quarter, he dialed.

"Let me speak to Beckman."

"Yeah?"

"Mr. Beckman, it's me, Joseph Sherman."

"Who?"

"Sherman from sports."

"Who?"

"Quips and Quotes."

"Oh, right. How are you? I'm awfully busy."

"I just spoke with Mr. Henry before he went to the airport. He wants me to follow up on a special assignment."

"What are you talking about?"

"I have an interview, and then I'm supposed to report directly back to you this afternoon."

"What's the story?"

Joseph paused, drew a breath and said, "Center Street" and quickly hung up.

A mahogany roll-top desk occupied the front corner of the living room. It was a second-floor, one-bedroom, west Greenwich Village, Bohemian-style apartment. Joseph lived alone. He loved calm colors and plants, especially ferns and philodendrons. His other passion was an assortment of tropical fish in three fifty-gallon tanks with blue-green, oceanic lighting.

Entering the room, Joseph plopped down on the sofa. Graduating first in his class at CCNY with a B.A. in literature, he had held four other jobs before landing the position at the Herald. Though they loved him, his family and friends referred to him as everything from lazy to laid-back to groundless. And admittedly so, until he had heard the rumors about Hudson.

Reaching down to the coffee table, he played the messages on his answering machine.

"Jose, Vance here. Can you get me two tickets to the Knicks-Lakers game? Name your price. Let me know."

"Hi, Joey. This is your adorable, gorgeous, precious sister. I'm having them over for lunch on Sunday. Please be here to keep the peace. Love you. Call me."

Joseph dialed her. "Hi, adorable, gorgeous, precious, modest one. What's up?"

"You have to help me, Joey. Mom was here yesterday and I made the mistake of telling her about the burglary across the street. Now, she's pressuring me to move back to Brooklyn Heights. I'm 35-years-old and not a cripple. They're coming over Sunday. Will you please be here? Will you?"

"What do you think?"

"I think you'll be here."

"You think right."

"You're the greatest."

"So are you. See you on Sunday."

"See ya."

Joseph hung up the phone and pushed the button to continue the messages.

·⁀·

"Hi, darling, it's Cara. I just wanted to thank you for last night. I'm still tingling. You're wonderful. I love you. Call me."

·⁀·

Joseph felt indifferent about Cara, as well as the other women he was dating. Three months earlier he had broken up with the love of his life. Barbara was intelligent, independent, mature and deeply in love with him. She wanted marriage, but Joseph insisted he wasn't ready. That is he wasn't until Barbara left New York and disappeared.

Lifting the phone he called Cara. "Hi. I got your message."

"And I got one from you last night."

"What?"

"I think; no, I'm sure we love each other, darling. It's been two months. I think we should think about living together."

"I'm sorry, Cara, but I'm not ready to live with you or anyone else."

"I'm not just anyone."

"You're not?"

"Stop kidding around, Joseph."

"I'm not kidding. You're a wonderful girl, but my head is still screwed up. I simply don't have time for love right now. Nothing personal."

"Screw you!"

"Oooh, Cara, I asked you not to take it personally."

Joseph heard the phone slam down on the other end. After replacing his receiver, he pressed the button to hear the rest of the messages.

·⁀·

"Joseph, this is your mother." He laughed because he knew what was coming. *"I'm worried about Debbie. We've simply got to get her out of that neighborhood. She's invited us over for lunch on Sunday. Please be there to help me talk to her."*

·⁀·

"Joe, this is Sidney. You are one lame dude for not coming to my party last night. There was a scrumptious dancer here with the most

perfect set of legs that God ever set forth. And that's not all. The prettiest green eyes, face, tits, ass and everything poured into the tightest dress I have ever seen. And get this...she was asking about you. You goofed, baby. I gave her your number. Oh, yeah, before I forget. See if you can get me some Islanders-Rangers tickets and I'll forgive you. Let me know."

"Sherman, this is Beckman. Don't be a schmuck! Stay away from that story, and call me if you want to keep your job."

"Joseph, hi." It was a mature woman's voice. *"We spoke last week concerning Hudson. There is a special name and person you should be aware of. It's Junie Sando."*

Joseph ran the tape back just enough to hear, "It's Junie Sando."
Checking his watch, Joseph realized he was running late.
The phone rang. "Hello."
There was a pause, and then a male's voice asked, "You're still there?"
"Who is this?"
"You don't want to be late for the interview."
"I won't be."

Entering the lobby of the Pierre Hotel and going up to the desk, Joseph asked for Teddy West. He learned he was in suite 2804 and that Mr. West was expecting him. In the elevator, Joseph checked to make certain the recorder was working. He got this far because someone telephoned at daybreak saying, "If you would like some pertinent information about the Hudson incident, meet me at the Pierre Hotel at nine-thirty in the morning."
Joseph did as directed. A tall, raven haired, model-type with hostile blue eyes, was waiting in the lobby. He said that he could arrange an interview with Mr. Teddy West at noon.
"Will I get everything?"
"People usually get what they deserve."
"Is that one of your family sayings?"
"You'll find out."
"What about Tuck Ryan?"
"Who do you want to interview, Mr. West or me?"

"Mr. West."

"Then I suggest you get a move on and return here no later than twelve o'clock."

"One more quick question. Could you give me an estimate of how many people were...terminated?"

When the man merely glared impatiently at him, Joseph said he must speak with his boss and left the hotel.

Stepping from the elevator now, Joseph took a quick breath and walked up to suite 2804. The door was cracked open. When he knocked, it moved further.

"I think you'd better come on in," said a voice from inside the room. Entering cautiously, Joseph was amazed at the opulence of the suite. Decorated with Edwardian furniture, the color scheme was Wedgewood blue. There was an awesome view of the picturesque landscape of Central Park. He estimated that the suite went for no less than $1,000 a day. And draped over the back of one of the chairs was a man's fur-lined trench coat, exactly like the one the woman wore in Hudson. The voice that invited him in now called from the other room, saying he was coming right out. A handsome, middle-aged black man in a pin-striped, tailor-made suit and silk shirt and tie, entered the room. He was not at all what Joseph expected.

"You're Mr. West?"

"Put your eyes back in your head, boy."

"Are you the real Center Street strategist?"

"My title was War Counselor back then. Do you think they only come in white?"

"Of course not."

"I can understand your surprise," Teddy said, and then went on to explain that there were only two hundred black people and over eight thousand whites in Hudson in 1958. "We had a choice of either segregating or integrating. I, and a few others, chose the latter and there was almost no trouble about it. However, Hudson was ethnically divided before Center Street. Most of the Italians were in the southwest corner near the river and south of the Blacks. The Poles were along the north end of town. Frog Bottom was directly south in the swamp, and the Irish were midtown. The WASPS and the few Jewish families were on the east and wealthier end of town. Mind if I call you Sherm?"

"Not at all."

Asking Joseph to have a seat, Teddy waited for him to sit before deciding where he wanted to be. Joseph chose one of the chairs. Teddy reclined on a sofa directly across from him.

"You want a drink or something, Sherm?"

"No, thank you."

"I understand a lot of people have warned you against investigating this story."

"I might lose my job because of it."

"You wouldn't want to do that, would you?"

"You are going to give me the interview, aren't you?" When Teddy merely stared at him, Joseph asked, "I am getting the interview, aren't I?"

"To tell the truth, Sherm, some people feel that the story should just die where it happened."

"Goddammit, I knew you weren't Teddy West! Who the hell are you, some kind of hit man?"

"I've never committed an act of violence in my entire life."

"You're supposed to be their general, their war counselor."

"Generals don't kill...personally."

"Who are you!?" Joseph shouted in anger.

Calmly, Teddy reached into his inside coat pocket, brought out his wallet and flapped it open to his driver's license.

"All right, so you're you. Why can't I have the story?"

"What if I tell you that knowing the story could cause you more harm than good?"

"It has already caused me more harm than you can imagine."

"All we want is for you to stop prying."

"Who are we? Are you guys still organized?"

"Organized is a very establishment and certified-type of word. We're friends, old and young, with certain things in common."

"Like what?"

"Well, for instance, you, Sherm. We have you in common. And we have a collective desire for you to mind your own damn business."

"I will as soon as I know what happened in Hudson. Besides, reporting is my business."

Teddy hesitated long enough to chuckle. "Quips and Quotes? I have to admit I admire your gumption, Sherm. We could have used you back then."

"Tell me the story, Mr. West. Please."

Teddy smiled and said, "There are some very definite ways to tell just how badly you want to be a hard rock reporter, investigator, Broadway, Times Square, Pulitzer Prize and the whole shot."

"Do I get the interview if I pass the test?"

"You pass this test and you'll become a bona fide member of Center Street."

"Then let's do it," Joseph said. "This story means more to me than anything else."

Teddy smiled and shook his head. "Okay." He lifted the phone, got an outside line, dialed a number and said, "Hi, it's me. He's here. He wants it and...I think he'll do. Speak to you later." Placing the receiver down, Teddy removed his jacket and loosened his tie. "Let's get on it, Shermie."

Joseph placed the small GE tape recorder on the coffee table. "I'm going to turn on the tape now and start the interview."

Chuckling, Teddy said, "You're a 'blip,' Sherm."

Joseph nodded and then pushed the record button.

Joseph: "I'm sorry to begin on such a harsh note, but what made you people even think of starting such an organization?"

Teddy: "Before you become too judgmental, and I'm not making excuses for what we did, keep it all in perspective,
Sherm. The gambling and the whores were a financial
bonanza. We were just small-town hicks making the best
of a bad situation. The whole business only lasted seven
weeks. We had no idea it would go so far and become the
brutal reality that still, this many years later, haunts so
many of us. The rumors continue and the exaggerations
of what really happened grow larger with each telling."

Mary Granelli was one of those dark-eyed beauties who is distinctly Neapolitan. She was eighteen back in 1958, extremely intelligent and constantly being referred to as "stacked." She and Junie
Sando were sitting quietly in the last booth of Zeito's soda shop on
the corner of Main and Fifth Streets. Mary was listening to Tony
Bennett's "Because of You" playing on the jukebox. Junie was staring into space, preoccupied with something that was causing him
to be unusually quiet. Mary knew him well enough, loved him
more than enough to know something was wrong. But rather than
press him on it, she held his head against her breasts, brushed his

black hair away from his baby face and let him know she was available whenever and for whatever he needed.

Directly across the street from Zeito's, at the end of a row of houses that were covered with colorful tar shingles, was another soda shop. This one was frequented by the Irish Hawks. There were more than a dozen boys sitting on the front steps. Some were admiring Junie Sando's customized, silver Studebaker that was being fitted for white sidewall tires at the Fifth Street Garage.

As Mary and Junie crossed the street, the Hawks watched them closely without a word. Some were tempted to say something. Perhaps compliment Junie on his car. Maybe a few wanted to just say, "Hi," but were afraid it might be taken the wrong way. One boy, a kid named Stucko, watching the way Mary's shapely body flowed in the breeze and glistened in the sunlight, wanted to make a comment, or maybe even give a little whistle, but he didn't. Junie Sando didn't look as if he was in such a good mood, so the Hawks remained silent.

Opening the car door for Mary, Junie glanced over the top of the Studebaker. He closed the door and then turned to the mechanic, paid him and walked around to the driver's side. Stopping there, he waited as if daring the Hawks to attack his back.

The leader, Kevin Boone, rose from the center of his boys. He was accompanied by one of his warriors who was dressed in leather with a chain wrapped around his hand with its deadly, jagged end dangling a foot down. Junie could feel the boys approaching him and remained with his back to them.

"We want a pow-wow," Kevin said.

Junie turned. "What?"

"A two-on-two. Me and Spike Danner here against you and Danny Tiano."

Junie chuckled and said, "You just think you do."

"We want it."

"It's an odd request," said Junie.

"Why?"

"Because Danny Tiano can beat the crap out of both of you with one hand tied behind his back."

"Time, place and weapons?" Kevin demanded.

"Nineteen ninety-nine, Miami with snowballs," Junie said and stepped into the Studebaker and drove away.

Danny Tiano, nineteen, was a tall, dark, able and dangerous tough of Roman descent. He and Junie Sando had been inseparable friends practically from the moment they were born. The two families lived next door to each other on First Street. Their mothers were like sisters and used to sit on the front stoops with their bambini on their laps while discussing the choice gossip of the day. As toddlers the boys shared the sandbox on Parade Hill Park. They started kindergarten together, played Little League, joined the River Rats at age thirteen and fought back-to-back against the other gangs. They agreed to switch over to Center Street when they were sixteen, and the following summer they graduated from Hudson High School. The very first iota of any trouble between them came that same year. Her name was Carol Tanner, an intelligent but plain, frail girl from a frowned on little hick town twenty miles northeast of Hudson.

"Nobody dates a girl from Philmont," Junie said, half-kidding, to which Danny replied, "I do."

Some of the tougher Center Street Debs attempted to scare Carol away. Junie, realizing how serious Danny was about her, put an immediate stop to the threats, threw a party in her honor and introduced Carol Tanner as a bona fide member of Center Street. This smoothed things over very quickly. However, with both boys going steady, it gave them a valid reason for spending less time together, even though they did double-date occasionally during the next two years.

On a musty, overcast day in late August of 1958, Danny Tiano sent for Junie. He and Carol were playing Scrabble in the living room. The tasty smells of parmesan and lasagna were emanating from his mother's kitchen. When Junie and Mary arrived, the four of them greeted each other pleasantly with Junie and Danny smiling at each other as always. Carol then guided Mary out of the room.

Junie waited. After a minute, Danny proudly announced, "Carol and me, we're getting hitched the third Sunday of next month."

Junie smiled, shrugged and said, "Okay."

"You think I'm out of my mind, right?"

"Well, nineteen is a bit...young and childish."

"No. I'll tell you what's childish. Center Street is childish."

"I think Center Street's been pretty good to you."

"I didn't say it hasn't. I just don't want to belong to a gang anymore."

"We're not a gang."

"I know, I know, you're a business," Danny said. "You own a few properties, collect some rents, and some dues, and the members are hustling and guiding the tourists to the whorehouses and the casinos. So, are you going to do this stuff in this town forever? You said you wanted to be a priest at one time." Danny winked at him and added, "Until you met Mary. Look, I'm not knocking you, I just want you to understand me. We're best friends. Hell, I'll admit I like being your number one warrior, but I'm no fool. I know damn well that any time you wanted to, you could have beat the crap out of me."

"That's not necessarily true."

"It doesn't matter. I'd rather have my hands cut off than use them on you. But Center Street is a toy, and it's time to put our toys away."

Junie stared at Danny for a moment. "Why don't you quit stalling and tell me what you're really going to do."

Danny looked away, cleared his throat and said, "All right. Nick Coletti has offered me a job, and I'm going to take it. Besides that, he's going to open up another casino next year. If I play my cards right, I just might be in line to manage the new place. And get this. Once I'm in tight, do you know what I'm going to do? Bring in my best friend."

"I don't want to work for them. I hate Nick. We own Diamond Street, and they're telling us to keep our guys from in front of their buildings. That's bullshit!"

"Junie, this whole town is making money off Nick. Including Center Street, especially Center Street."

"So what? Don't you remember when we said we would never stoop that low? Be a part of a Mob? What's happened to you?"

"I want this job, and I'm going to take it. I'm going to be a married man with responsibilities. I don't feel like working at one of those cement plants, getting my lungs all screwed up and dropping dead at fifty. Or becoming an apple- knocker and picking fruit for ten cents a bucket. I want this job."

"Then take it."

"I am."

"You know, don't you," Junie said, "that there are some guys who think we can run Nick out and take over his operations?"

"That would really be unhealthy, Junie."

"You sound as if you're already on their side."

"There are no sides! There's no war between you and Nick Coletti. Live and let live. Say you run Nick out, the next day the Don will send thirty hoods up here from the city to take their place. You can't beat them."

"Maybe," Junie said and stood. "Once you're in, you tell them that the Second Street parking lot is ours. The next time they run some of my guys off, they're going to pay."

"Junie, for chrissake, what the hell are you talking about? Parking lots, kids in front of buildings...?"

"This is our town, not theirs."

Danny paused. "I love you, Junie, and I swear to God I do, but if I start working for Nick and you decide to take Center Street against them...you see where that puts us."

"You're making the choice," Junie said and went to the front door. "Mary!"

When Mary came into the room, Junie and Danny were staring coldly at each other.

"You know something?" Danny said, wryly. "For the first time in a long time I wish we were on our way to the sandbox again."

"Maybe we are," Junie said and opened the door for Mary.

2

Joseph: "So, Junie, Danny and you were the three main members of Center Street?"

Teddy: "In the beginning that's the way it was. Junie and I could always talk. But to tell the truth, I was surprised at his reaction when I first mentioned the idea of Center Street. He didn't laugh at me, or tell me to go take a hike. He simply said that we should both give it a lot of thought."

The upper Hudson River Valley is in its full, dark green glory during the summer months. But upstate New York is such a tranquil and bountiful part of the country that the valley can be breathtaking any time of year. Even in the bitter cold of winter when the virgin snows are drifting three or four feet high. Or in the spring when the pink and white apple and cherry blossoms adorn the rolling landscapes. And, of course, there is autumn, the most pastoral of seasons. However, all of this is merely the dressing. The sterling centerpiece of the valley is the river. The wide, noble, soft-flowing Hudson River that is born mysteriously up in the Adirondack Mountains and then winds its way directly south.

There was no better place to view all of this than on Parade Hill at the base of the city of Hudson. The grassy park, towering on a two-hundred-foot, black rock cliff, stood like a paper fortress against the entire world, formidable yet vulnerable. At best it was a juvenile citadel, the river its moat, the height its challenge and defense. From the edge, a child could look down on the universe with visions of grandeur and invincibility. But the park, fashioned delicately with colorful flower beds, manicured lawns and white gravel walkways, was only a place to rest, to view, to escape, or to dream.

Junie Sando and Teddy West met there in private several times before deciding to put Center Street into action by gathering some of the best and the brightest boys and girls from all the other neighborhoods. Because most of the members of the new club lived in the center of town; and because they claimed the middle of the city, two blocks wide, they became known as "Center Street."

(In actuality, there was no avenue,
nor boulevard or thoroughfare of
any sort by the name of Center
Street in the city of Hudson).

Teddy West thought of himself as a military strategist, and he became the war counselor. He was also a constant loner and Parade Hill Park was his sanctuary to relax, read or simply be alone. When Junie Sando walked up now, the two of them were silhouetted against the mystical, dark green rolls of the Catskill Mountains. Junie leaned on the spiked fence that edged the park. Teddy could tell something was wrong for two reasons. One, Junie wasn't smiling; and two, he wasn't talking.

"Let's hear it."

Junie explained that Danny Tiano was not only quitting and getting married, but was joining up with Nick Coletti. Teddy didn't expect the latter, but tried to make light of it. "Hey, I wouldn't worry about it. Once a member of Center Street, always a member. You know that."

"Frank Borzak and some of the Streeters think we can chase Nick and his bunch out and take over."

Teddy chuckled. "Frank came to me with that idea, and I told him to forget it. If he thinks it's so easy, why doesn't he do it with the Robinson Street Reds. They're twice as big as we are."

"You know we're the only ones who can do it, Teddy."

"But we have nothing to gain and everything to lose. Even if we took over, how long would we last before Albany got the word and sent the State Troopers in to close us down? Nick has connections to keep John Law off his back. We don't. We'd just be hurting ourselves."

"How?"

"First of all, Nick and especially Lido Sandrelli are not going to give up a million-dollar operation without one hell of a fight."

"We out-number them."

"Junie...get it out of your mind. Without Nick this town is nothing. Without the casinos, the cat houses and tourists we got ourselves a ghost town. I know you're upset with Danny, but if we need him, he'll help us. Believe me. Look, school starts next Monday. Everything will be cool until way next summer."

Junie gave it some thought, nodded and said, "You better be right...for their sakes."

Even though Junie had mixed emotions about being Danny's best man, he agreed to it. However, once the huge, religious wedding was over, he and Mary Granelli left St. Mary's Church and drove away without attending the reception. Danny was naturally hurt by this. He decided to wait until a week after they returned from their two-week honeymoon at Niagara Falls to call him on it.

"Why didn't you come to our reception?"

Junie merely shrugged.

"It's traditional that the best man give the toast," Danny explained. "Junie, Junie, Junie, don't you ever forgive and forget?"

"There's nothing to forgive, Danny."

"Well, if it makes you feel any better, I'm not making nearly as much money as I thought I would. Nick's a cheap bastard. We're okay now because of the money we got at the reception. But the payments on our house are going to be rough to meet every month, especially with Carol already pregnant."

"She got pregnant on the honeymoon?" Junie asked.

"Nahh, she missed her period the month before. It's all right. We were going to get married anyway."

"Don't you think you should wait before starting a family?"

"Carol really wants it. We'll find a way to make it."

"Danny, I'm serious. I may be a jerk when it comes to receptions, but I'll always be in your corner."

"We'll see."

Autumn seems to rush by in upstate New York. Perhaps because the fall is so pleasant and pretty, and the harsh winter looms like some menacing ogre threatening to ride in on the very next cloud.

The first snow fall that year, though light, managed to cover the dark roof of the main school building. It lasted only during the morning hours because the sun, still attempting to sizzle like summer, burned away the clouds and turned the snow into running slush.

The second floor of Hudson High had polished floors. The halls were lined with student lockers built into dark brown and beige tiles. At the far end were two, large doors leading to the study hall. Waiting with Augie Sando, a short, fat, curly-headed Italian boy, was Butch Charles, a happy-go-lucky black kid. Both were seventeen and cracking on each other.

"I heard," Augie was saying, "that when you was born, you was so ugly that the doctor slapped your motha' instead of you."

"Oh, yeh," said Butch. "Well, I heard that when you was hatched, you was so ugly the doctor had to paint a red circle around your mouth so your momma would know where to shove the dog food."

"Hardeeharhar," Augie said.

The boys laughed but stopped when someone came up to them. "Hi, guys." It was Janet Hammond. One of the school's brightest students, but not one of its beauties.

"Hey, Janet, you seen Frank Borzak?" Butch asked.

"He's probably in study hall. Why?"

"None of your business!" Augie shouted.

"We're just making friends," Butch explained. "What else could it be?"

"I don't know, but I'll find out."

"Okay," said Butch. "When you find out somethin', let us know."

"Don't worry, I will."

Frank Borzak, a tall, tough, snarl of a boy with a crew cut, sat hunched over a science book. His scholastic average was third only to Janet Hammond and Marty Politzsky.

"Studyin' hard?" Butch Charles asked. He and Augie took seats across from Frank.

"Hardly studying," Frank replied. "What's the word?"

"The Streeters won't make a move without Junie."

"Shit!"

"It's a lost cause, Frank. We agree with you, but what can we do?"

"So Junie is the only thing that's holding us up?"

"He ain't gonna do it," Butch said. "Besides, it's winter. Nobody wants to do nothin' in the winter. Let's talk about it next summer."

"We have to prepare for next summer if we're going to do it next summer. We could be rich by next summer."

"Like I said, you can't do it without Center Street, and Junie is Center Street."

Butch and Augie got up then to leave.

Hudson High School broke at two-thirty in the afternoon. Every day Frank Borzak could be seen walking the ten blocks to Robinson Street. He was crossing Third when he jumped a large gutter of slush. It was normal weather for middle December: snow flurries, some bitter cold winds, and an occasional rain which the frigid air could turn into hazardous ice slicks.

Frank was dressed warmly in floppy galoshes, corduroy trousers, navy pea coat, scarf and a knit hat. He was not a completely evil boy. If he had been asked to describe that word, he would instantly say that the local hoods, Nick Coletti or, more likely, Lido Sandrelli were the essence of evil. Frank wasn't even a mean person. It was simply that he was so bright, so full of lofty ideas and ambitions that his mind was always in high drive. He wanted to change the world, make it better, rebuild it to his specifications, even if his philosophy was warped, socialistic, communistic and, not in the least, narcissistic. In a nice way, Junie Sando once told him, "You think too much, Frank. Try not to think so hard."

As Frank crossed State Street, a 1950 Chevy convertible screeched to a halt at the curb. Two boys jumped out, one doubled him up with a kick in the belly, and they threw him into the car. It was the Robinson Street Reds way of saying they wanted to have a chat with you.

The leader of the Reds was a large, bald-headed Bolshevik by the name of Boris Robanski, twenty-one, who sat at the center of the council table with his lieutenants at his side. Frank was placed in front of the basement table and accused of "Fraternizing with the enemy."

"How do you plead?"

While holding his gut, Frank was still trying to catch his breath.

"Silence is an admission of guilt," a loud-mouthed lieutenant shouted.

Wanting to plead his case only to Boris, Frank said, "There is something I can't talk about except to you alone."

"What in the hell have you been telling them?" the loudmouth barked at Frank.

"Nothing about us."

"Did you tell them our plan?"

"What plan? I don't know anything about any damn plan."

Boris reminded him that Frank wasn't at the last meeting.

"He could have found out from one of our other members," the lieutenant warned.

"What are you talking about?" Frank said.

Boris leaned forward and asked, "Did you know we were planning an all-out winter raid on the Streeters?"

Frank was shocked. He looked from one member to the other in disbelief and then laughed, "You're kidding?"

"No, we're not kidding," said the lieutenant.

Continuing to chuckle, Frank said, "They'll kill you."

"Not if we surprise them."

"Surprise them with what?! Even if you surprised them and hurt them, they'd come back at you with everything they've got. In case you haven't noticed, Center Street doesn't lose rumbles, and they've got everything they need and more to wipe you guys out."

"They're stepping out of line," one member complained.

"They're getting too powerful," shouted another.

"We gotta cut 'em down to size."

"Boris," Frank pleaded, "will you please get these clowns out of here so I can talk to you?"

When two toughs grabbed Frank and were about to do him in, Boris ordered them to stop. "Give me five minutes with him. If he's got nothing to say, you can have him."

Reluctantly, the other members moved out of the cellar clubhouse. Some deliberately bumped Frank as they passed. Once they were alone, Frank moved to the table and began, "All right, Boris, here it is. I've got a plan where I'm going to get Center Street to go against Nick Coletti."

"What are you, nuts?"

"They can do it. You know you don't want to rumble with the Streeters, Boris."

"Did Junie agree to this?"

"Not yet."

"How are you going to get him to do something like that?"

"Let me worry about that?"

"I guess if anybody can do it, you can. You've always been a sneaky little bastard."

"As long as I get the job done, what difference does it make?"

"You really think you can do it?"

"We're going to do it...if you can manage to keep those jerkballs off my back. What do you say?"

"This better be on the level, Frank."

"Not only am I being on the level with you, but when the time comes, when the time is exactly right, we're going to get it all."

Boris chuckled. "You'll have to kill Junie, Danny Tiano and maybe even Teddy West, too."

"No. Teddy doesn't want anything to do with it. And get this, Danny has already gone over to Nick."

"What?"

"That's right. And Junie is pissed."

"Don't count on that, Frank. Anything happens to Junie Sando, Danny's going to start killing people and he won't stop until he gets the right one."

"As long as he doesn't come after us, I don't care how much they fight amongst themselves. We'll just sit back and let Center Street do all the dirty work, and then I'll find a way to get all that power in the palm of my hand."

"You're an ambitious little punk, ain't you?"

"Ambitious, yes. Punk, no. I've always said that whoever gets it, deserves it. I'll report back to you directly. But do me a favor and talk to those maniacs out there, will you, please?"

Boris smiled and nodded.

3

Teddy: "You damn right we were afraid of Danny Tiano being with Nick. But I still believed he would come back to us. There was nothing and no one in this world that could ever make Junie and Danny fight against each other."

Late one frigid night in the middle of March 1959, Danny Tiano telephoned Junie Sando. "Are you sleeping?"

"No, I'm always up at three-thirty in the morning."

"Did I wake anybody else?"

"It's okay, Pop," Junie said to his father who came to the bedroom door. Mr. Sandolini, dressed only in pajama bottoms, shook his head, yawned and went back to bed.

"Is your father pissed?"

"No, he loves being disturbed in the middle of the night when he has to get up at six o'clock to go to work."

"This is important, Junie."

"It better be."

"I've been chipping."

Junie was shocked. "Are you crazy, Danny?"

"They can't catch me. I handle all the receipts. I just burn a few and pocket the cash."

"You think Nick doesn't know how many receipts are being used?"

"I don't take that much. No more than ten, fifteen bucks a night, and not every night. Do you have any idea how much money they're making? They took in close to twenty grand last week. Do you believe that in a town this small?"

"Wasn't there a bowlers' convention last weekend?"

"Right. But imagine the business Nick's going to do this summer."

"Great. I'm happy for Nick, but what does this have to do with me at three-thirty in the morning?"

"I'm the cashier, Junie. I take the money from the cashier's cage to the office safe at this time every night. If two masked men were to come in the back door and stick me up, they could get away easily. Bobby West and Jeff Gershon could do it."

"You really think I'm going to put those guys' lives on the line for you?"

"I need the money, Junie. Carol's been having problems. She has to go to the doctor all the time. And the house payments, the car. Come on, buddy, let's do it."

"If you need money, Danny, you come to us."

"I need a hell of a lot more than you can give me."

"You don't know that. Why don't you ask and find out."

Danny was quiet for a moment. "All right. I just thought this would be an easy way."

"I won't risk those guys on this, Danny. Not even for you. And if you're smart, you'll stop chipping before they catch your ass."

"I'm not worried about that."

"Come to us, Danny. Please come back to us."

After a pause, Danny said he would be in touch.

Very seldom did Junie and Mary discuss Carol and Danny. It came up on April 7, 1959. They were in Junie's bedroom while his parents were at Saturday afternoon bingo. They made love. Junie's passions were holding and kissing as well as all the rest, whereas Mary was seized, mesmerized by intercourse. Especially the climaxing, which she enjoyed repeatedly.

Junie was partial to Mary's breasts, her long, smooth thighs and her flower-soft, honey lips. Mary, on the other hand, simply loved Junie, every inch of him, and she made love to all of him while often becoming frantic, mildly hysterical, but always remaining passionate.

They rested now. Junie against the head board, Mary leaning

back on him. She allowed her joy and elation to conjure up incessant fears about the future. For some reason, all the negative cliches she had ever heard (too good to be true, count your blessings, nothing lasts forever), would come to her at these moments. She didn't understand why it happened, yet something kept telling her that some day, in some way, Junie would be snatched from her. Mary closed her eyes and frowned in an attempt to erase those bleak thoughts. Brushing at her disheveled hair, she turned abruptly to kiss Junie. When he asked if everything was all right, she didn't reply.

Forcing a smile, Mary reminded Junie that Danny's baby was due in a week.

"I know. I really don't want to talk about it."

"Okay," she said. "Did you hear what happened with the basketball team on the bus coming back from the play-offs?"

"No."

"Well, you know Helene Mulzer."

"The big, beautiful blonde?"

"She's not that beautiful."

"The big blonde?"

"Right. Her. She made a bet with the star of Hudson that if they beat Albany High for first place, she would make-out with the entire starting five."

Junie started chuckling.

"As you know, Hudson upset Albany in double overtime. So coming home, the first string all sat on the back seat of the bus. And there was old Helene keeping her end of the bargain. She had worked her way up to the third guy, which of course, put her right in the aisle. Right then, the big redhead, Skippy McDonald, goes up in back of Helene, lifts her skirt and goes at her from the rear. And then Butch Charles goes up to the bus driver and tips him a buck to switch on the lights. Well, let me tell you, all hell broke loose. One of the other cheerleaders sees what's going on, starts screaming and this causes a chain reaction. Most of the kids were falling asleep. Miss Belli, the girls' gym teacher, who's in charge of the cheerleaders, is sitting in front of the bus. She screams the loudest. The driver, for some reason, slams on his breaks and everybody falls to the floor."

Junie was laughing so hard, he was crying.

"Would you believe nothing happened to the guys. But they

kicked poor Helene off the cheerleading squad and suspended her from school."

"That's sick," said Junie. Taking Mary into his arms he continued to chuckle.

They lay silent for a while, and then Mary said, "A penny for your thoughts."

"It's nothing."

"Come on, tell me."

"I'm...I'm worried about Danny. He's been chipping at Nick's. Says it's only ten or fifteen bucks at a time, but I'm sure it's more than that, or it will be."

"God, he must be crazy."

"I told him I would give him money if he'd come back to us. Hell, I'd even pay him more than Nick is if he'd come back."

"Why won't he?"

"He says he's legit now. And then in the next breath he wants us to pull a stickup like two-bit hoods. Dammit, we've got to rise above this somehow. You know what I think? I think Marty Politzsky is the one. He could raise us above being just a gang. He could show us how to be a business, a corporation."

"Teddy West is second-in-command. Won't he be upset?"

"No. Teddy is the perfect number-two man. He doesn't want to be a target. Marty's the one. He's smart, sensible, and he's a big kid. And he and Teddy could keep it from turning violent. I've got to find a way to get him in."

"You want me to talk to him?"

"No. I'll find a way."

The telephone rang at that moment, and Junie kissed Mary before answering it. "Hello."

"Junie?"

"What's wrong, Carol?"

"Can you come over here?"

"What is it?"

"Just get over here."

Within seconds Junie was up, dressed and leaving Mary sitting nude in the center of the bed. It took him less than five minutes to drive from Second and Diamond to Sixth and Union Streets. Danny Tiano had purchased a plain, brown-shingled, one-family house. As Junie ran up to the front door, he was suddenly gripped with a fear of what was inside. Carol heard him arrive and opened the door. Her eyes were red, swollen. Her hair was pinned hurriedly back. She was dressed warmly in boots and jeans with a sweater and blouse. As Junie entered the house, Carol closed and locked the door. Junie instantly noticed the packed boxes.

"You guys going somewhere?" he asked, fearfully.

"I am."

"Don't tell me you broke up."

Carol sat on the sofa while trying desperately not to cry. "I've got to look after my baby."

Junie sat close to her. This brought tears to Carol's eyes, and she moved away.

"What is it, Carol? Tell me!"

"He's gone," Carol said, barely coherent.

"Gone? Gone where?"

Tears were now trickling down her cheeks. "He got a phone call yesterday. It was his day off. He called you right away, but you weren't home. Then he said he would be right back. I knew he wouldn't."

"Who called him?" Junie asked.

"I don't know."

"Was it Nick?"

"He didn't say. But he didn't come home all night. I've got to think about my baby."

"Maybe he's sick or hurt somewhere," Junie offered feebly.

"Do you really believe that?"

All Junie could do was close his eyes.

"God, I hate this town," Carol exclaimed. "You're all so crazy with your gangs and your gangsters and your..."

"I'll find him, Carol."

"His corpse, you mean?"

"Noooo!"

"He's dead. You know it, and I know it."

"No!" Junie repeated.

"I'm getting the hell out of here," Carol said. "This is shit city. Philmont isn't much, but it sure beats the hell out of this scum hole." Carol reached into her bag and pulled out an envelope. "Here. It's the mortgage on this house. If you want to finish the payments, it's yours. And you can definitely have that."

Junie turned to see what Carol was pointing at. It was a large, sterling silver punch bowl. A wedding present from Nick Coletti and completely useless to Danny and Carol.

"How are you going to get to Philmont?" Junie asked.

"My mother's coming for me."

"Did you call the police?"

"The police!? What for? Even if I told them who I thought did it, what would they do? Nothing. You know that."

Junie nodded. "Carol, please wait. He might show up."

"Don't you know that if I thought there was one chance in a million, I wouldn't even think about leaving. Get out of this town, Junie. Get out of here before they kill you, too. It's not worth it. Nothing here is worth it. Get out. Take Mary and you guys go somewhere and have a dozen babies. You're both too damn good for this place."

"Not until I find out what happened to Danny."

Carol shook her head and said, "Then it'll be too late."

Junie kissed Carol on the cheek, said, "God bless you and the baby," and then got up and rushed out of the house.

Spring is new. It's clean, warm, fresh and extraordinarily beautiful in upstate New York. Frank Borzak, sensitive in his own way, appreciated the vernal season as much as anyone. He was returning from a long walk through one of the large blossoming apple orchards east of town when he felt something in the air. The usual rush and rowdiness of Hudson had fallen into a calm uneasiness. To Frank that wasn't necessarily bad. He sensed it was something good, and a definite anxiety began to build in him. As he reached the last block before his house, he began to run. Rushing in the front door just as the phone rang, he fought one of his teenage sisters for the receiver. "Hello."

"Frank?"

"Yes, Augie. What's up?"

"I think we got 'em, man."

"Give it to me."

"Danny Tiano is missing."

Frank took a seat, caught his breath and began to smile. "Thank God. Thank you, Jesus. What's Junie doing?"

"Cussin' and mad as hell."

"Good."

"Carol, Danny's wife, moved back to Philmont."

"Good riddance. Does Teddy West know yet?"

"Butch Charles went down to tell him."

"Terrific."

"Does this mean we start, Frank?"

"Not quite yet. Junie has to decide. But we might have to help him along."

"How?"

"We've got to try and find Danny's corpse."

"What? Where?"

"It's only one of two places. In the river or buried in the clay banks. I'm going to check the clay banks to see if there are any new diggings."

"Ain't you scared to go over there?"

"I'm not afraid of anything, Augie. When Junie calms down, tell him I'll meet him at eight o'clock tonight."

"Okay."

"We're on our way, Augie. History is about to be made in Hudson."

"How about makin' some money?"

"There's going to be more than you can spend in a lifetime."

"Now yer talkin'."

The adults of Hudson, nearly all hard-working, middle and lower class people, were mostly out of touch with what was happening. The word about Danny Tiano's disappearance was being passed from one teenager to the next. Talk was starting that Center Street would take revenge. Members from some of the other clubs were calling the Streeters, volunteering their services. Whoever answered the phone at the Streeters' clubhouse denied knowing anything about the situation, and no one knew the whereabouts of Junie Sando.

Teddy West, as usual, was up on Parade Hill Park. After Butch Charles told him about Danny, he cursed, kicked at the dirt, and waved Butch away. That afternoon, the sun labored through rank after rank of large bulbous clouds before resting behind the Catskill Mountains that formed the slumbering figure of Rip Van Winkle. As the sky turned a shade toward evening, leaving a purple haze, a purple mood, Teddy could feel the peace fleeing and the calm rumbling before the storm. He continued to curse while knowing full well that this was what he was living for, the big challenge, the battle against the unbeatable foe, the war he couldn't possibly win, but knew damn well they would win it. If there was a way they would prevail; but at what cost?

Hearing movement in back of him, Teddy turned. Gathered on the grassy knoll above the white gravel walkway were a few Warriors of Center Street. Boys he had trained. Together they had fought every gang in Hudson as well as those in the surrounding towns, including Greenport, Catskill, and Philmont, and not once did they come close to losing. The Streeters couldn't even conceive of being defeated. In every rumble they were out-numbered, but their tactics, discipline and determination had seen them through. They had not only gone undefeated, but even now they stood poised, ready and willing to follow Junie without fear against Nick Coletti. Nick with his thugs, his power, his killers and their willingness and eagerness to murder without fear of reprisal from anyone. But with the marshaling of the Center Street Warriors, that could easily change.

There was still no word from anyone on the whereabouts of Junie Sando.

The Politzsky two-story home was on one of the prettiest streets of Hudson, Fairview Avenue, which ran out of town and into route 9W directly north to Albany. There was a well-kept lawn in front of the house with the inevitable white, fragile picket fence.

Mrs. Emma Politzsky was a petite, white-haired, traditional woman. Her father, Misha Berman, heard a Dusseldorf street-corner Nazi speak in 1934 and decided immediately it wasn't where he wanted to raise his family. Beautiful, blonde Emma Louise Berman was sixteen when her family of nine, including four boys and three girls, came to America and moved in with their cousins in Hudson, New York. Three years later, she was married to a young tailor, Morris Politzsky, who owned a small, independent couturier shop on Fifth and Diamond Streets. That same year she suffered her first of three miscarriages before finally giving birth in her thirties to a hardy, eight-pound baby boy who would be her one and only offspring.

When the doorbell rang, Emma expected anyone but the tall, gorgeous, dark-haired girl asking to speak with Martin. Emma Politzsky was a cautious woman, very protective of her family, especially her only child. She was also perceptive and presumed Mary Granelli had not come to harm her son, but instead was in need of him. So rather than questioning her the way she would any other stranger, she simply turned and went to fetch Martin.

While waiting impatiently, Mary could hear Marty and Mrs. Politzsky angrily discussing the situation in another part of the house.

When Marty entered the living room, he asked Mary to have a seat. Emma Politzsky stood across the hallway, deep in the afternoon shadows of the dining room. She was unnerved at the way Mary immediately took Martin's hand. Several girls had had crushes on him, but they were the lovely, local Jewish girls. Once in a while a pretty gentile would follow him home, but this girl was mature, different, special. This one could get whatever she wanted with the simple touch of her hand.

Emma remained staring at the two of them as they spoke quietly, privately. Mary even leaned closer to Martin as he started to nod in agreement with what she was saying or asking. Emma wanted to scream at Mary to unhand her son. Or burst into the room and demand that her pride and joy be returned to her. Instead she retreated to the kitchen and closed the door so she could neither see nor hear what was happening.

As it neared 7:30 p.m., there was still no word on Junie Sando. The concern that something had also happened to him was beginning to foment among the Streeters. Ever increasing numbers of soldiers were gathering on the grass behind Teddy West. He remained alone, looking out over the river while becoming more fearful by the minute. If Junie failed to show up, there would be no choice in the matter. Teddy would be forced to declare immediate war on Nick Coletti. Perhaps he could keep the boys in line and go at the hoods with some semblance of military order.

After checking the clay banks and finding no fresh diggings, Frank Borzak returned to town to learn that Junie Sando was also missing. Frank rushed down to the park to plead with Teddy to attack. Teddy warned him to back off and to keep his mouth shut.

Teddy continued to look out at the river just as a flat oil tanker with its night lights gleaming, cruised laboriously against the tide, heading toward Albany. Entwining his fingers, he began to pray silently that Junie would reveal himself.

There were other people praying at that moment. Praying, wailing in sorrow and utter hopelessness. Still others were kneeling, lighting candles and appealing to the image of the Blessed Virgin. The entire Tiano family, aunts, uncles, grandparents and cousins gathered at Danny's parents' home to console each other. The mother kept asking why her son. "Dio mio, perche mio figlio? Perche mio figlio?"

In the dining room a lone figure sat transfixed. He was staring at a shoe box in the center of the table. Its top was off with its grizzly contents lying exposed. Junie Sando, who had remained in this catatonic state since arriving, had been sitting in the same chair for the last few hours. He kept picturing how the Mob would tie Danny face-down to a table, stretch his arms out in front of him, scream at him, and beat him with a baseball bat from head to toe. If Danny passed out, they would wake him with a bucket of cold water. It wouldn't matter if he confessed. They weren't after a confession. They wanted revenge. And when they tired, and only then, would they mercilessly chop off his right hand, probably with a meat cleaver, and shoot him.

Danny Tiano's sister Angela, 17, came to the door and uttered, "They said he was chipping, Junie. I don't believe them. Momma and Poppa said he would never steal anything."

As Angela turned and rushed away, it brought Junie back to life. He stood up, looked down at Danny's severed hand that was grasping a fish, and said, "Chipping, huh? I swear to you, Danny, as God is my witness, they're going to wish they had never met you, hired you, or accused you of anything. Chipping, huh?" Junie placed the top on the box.

Coming out into the street, Junie found Mary Granelli and Marty Politzsky waiting for him. Marty simply stood there with his hands out, offering himself, heart and soul to whatever Junie wanted. "I don't know what I can do, but if you want me, if you need me, I'm yours."

Junie walked up to Marty and they embraced.

More soldiers had gathered on the grassy knoll now, and the latter ones were dressed for battle. Some had weapons. But there was one huge sigh of relief when Junie suddenly climbed up on the south end of the park and walked directly over to Teddy West.

"Where in the hell have you been?"

"Those bastards cut off Danny's hand, wrapped it around a mackerel and delivered it to his parents. Do you know what that means in Sicilian?"

"Of course. The hand is the one that stole from them, and it means Danny is at the bottom of the river."

"They said he was chipping."

"And he probably was," said Teddy. "Danny knew what the gig was when he took it, Junie."

"It doesn't matter. You know the one golden rule of Center Street. Any acts of terror against us must be returned in kind."

"Don't get mad if I remind you of something, but Danny quit us and joined up with Nick."

"I'm sure it was you, Teddy, who said 'once a member always a member.' Center Street's unyielding Motto is: **We Take Care of Our Own**, and you know what Danny would have done."

"But we're talking about murder."

"So what!?"

"God knows I don't want to do this, Junie."

"But God knows you will, for me...for Center Street."

"You know, don't you, that once something like this starts, it never stops? Never."

"They brought it on themselves."

While Teddy was contemplating what else he could possibly say to hold off the retaliations, Frank Borzak approached the two of them cautiously. Marty Politzsky also moved prudently into the group.

"We can do it," Frank said, softly. "We can get rid of them and take over their operations."

"Why don't we just run them out?" Marty asked. "Harass them. Hit them where it hurts, in their pockets, their casinos. Let's cut their telephone wires, jam their slot machines and flatten their tires. We'll drive them right out of their minds and out of Hudson."

When Frank Borzak complained that would take too long, Teddy said, "Not if we get on it right away. A week or two at the most."

"And suppose they kill another one of us?" Frank asked.

Everyone looked at Teddy. He paused and then said, "In that case I'll form up assassination squads and eliminate them one by one. But if we go running at them now, killing them off, we'll be no better than they are, and even worse because we know better. And we're bound to lose some of our own guys that way."

"Harassment is the way," Marty stated. "Mercilessly. Consistently. Day and night."

Teddy nodded to Junie, and said, "Who will you use?"

After a thought, Junie said, "Jeff Gershon, your brother Bobby, and Cat Killer."

"No, don't use Cat Killer. He's been going a little buggy lately. You, Jeff and Bobby can do what has to be done."

Junie said, "Teddy, I want you and Marty to talk to the gangs.

We don't need any rumbles while we're doing this."

"Why don't we bring them all into Center Street?" Teddy asked. "Form one, big efficient organization."

"Great idea," said Frank.

"We'll divide them into sections. Every teenage boy and girl will be assigned to a section. And we'll try to find jobs for everybody. If the kids aren't working for us, we'll find regular jobs for them somewhere else. They will be hired."

When Junie asked Marty what he thought, Marty began to nod in agreement. "Fine. But everything must be done non-violently."

"Of course," said Frank. "If we can."

"We can do it."

"We're going to do it, Marty," said Junie. "But I want those bastards out of this town by the first week of July at the very latest."

Frank said they would be...one way or another.

When Teddy stated he wanted to speak to Junie alone, Frank and Marty walked a short distance away.

While looking at the boys up on the grass, Teddy said, "I think you should speak to them."

"Not now. I'm not in the mood."

"Would you like to give a little thought to the kind of mood they're in?"

Junie looked at the boys.

"They're ready to die for you. The least you can do is say a few words on their behalf."

Lowering his head, Junie said, "I wouldn't know what to say."

"Then don't say anything. Just go stand amongst them. They'll understand."

"Did you ever think that sometimes you ask too much of me?"

"I've never asked you to do anything that is beyond your ability."

"But that doesn't mean you wouldn't."

"I truly understand the way you feel about Danny and what you're going through, but-"

"I don't think you do, and I don't think you give a damn."

"...but he's dead and those guys are more than willing to join him, but only for you. Only for you. Now, you have to respect that. Recognize that and do what's right. And what is right is to go up there this minute and tell them how you feel about them, because their being here demonstrates what they feel for you. You don't have to say a word. Just go there."

37

Junie glared disapprovingly at Teddy and shook his head in disgust. Then he turned and climbed the small, stone wall up to the lawn. Moving into the circle of teenagers, he squatted down. When one of the boys offered him a cigarette, he frowned. The kid quickly tucked it away. Another boy had a small bag of Planters Nuts and held them out to Junie. He reached into the bag, took out a single pea and chucked it up and down in the center of his palm.

After a moment, Junie gazed around at the boys. "My friend is dead. As far back as I can remember, Danny Tiano was always there for me. We grew up together, we loved each other. Many times we fought back-to-back, and I was never worried. Never. He was the greatest Warrior Center Street ever had...and now they have taken him from me. From us." Junie looked at the boys. "Why do they think so little of us? What do we have to do to gain their respect? Do we have to become like them? We have always desired peace, worked toward peace and even fought to maintain peace. God says to have patience and turn the other cheek. And I think we should. But I'm here to tell God and anyone else, that we only have two cheeks, and we are certainly running out of patience.

"This is your town. This is your home. Danny Tiano was our friend, our family. If we do not protect our homes and our families, then what are we? What are we? We can be whatever we have to be, from the very best to the most dangerous. They don't know like I know, that if they ever push us too far, they will unleash a power that will be terrible to behold. But until that time comes, we will remain prepared and strong. And I will never ask you to do anything that I would hesitate to do myself."

As Junie rose and walked out of the park, the soldiers packed up their weapons and began to disband. Teddy looked over at Frank, who was shaking his head in disbelief. Going over to him, Teddy said, "Isn't he incredible? And he thought he had nothing to say."

"You know as well as I do that sooner or later we're going to have to go to war. I say the sooner the better. We should surprise them. The element of surprise, 'General,' is one of the most significant advantages. If we lose that with them, we may very well lose the war."

"We have never lost a single battle, much less an entire war."

"There is always the first time, and with them it will be your last."

"You didn't say 'ours,'" Teddy said and chuckled.

Frank glared coldly at him before walking away.

4

Teddy: "Junie was fond of quoting someone when he'd say, 'Evil flourishes, Teddy, when good men do nothing.'"
Joseph: "Did you guys think of Junie as a god?"
Teddy: "Of course, not. There's only one God, and I wish He had taken a hand in what happened a lot sooner."

The silver Studebaker moved slowly, cautiously through the night, past the train station and down the narrow road to a long line of fortified, brick buildings. Junie parked in the blackness on the edge of Frog Bottom swamp. He, Bobby West and Jeff Gershon, all in dark clothing, sat and waited.

The night watchman made his rounds once an hour on the half-hour. It was now 10:30 p.m. Before the boys could hear or see him, they saw the beam of his flashlight strafing the sides of the buildings and stopping as he checked the padlocks on each storeroom. He was an old man, stooped and tired, and too frail to defend his charge. The three boys had no intention of putting him to that test. They waited until he was well past before they rushed up to the building. While Bobby held a small flashlight, Jeff Gershon examined the large, dependable padlock.

"Do you think you can open it?"

"Does a duck wear spats?" Jeff answered while taking a few metal instruments from his pocket. After fidgeting for a moment inside the mechanism, Jeff snapped open the lock. Once Junie and Bobby were inside, Jeff closed the door and replaced the lock. Silently, with flashlights in hand, Junie and Bobby moved into Nick Coletti's storage room to jam-up the slots with slugs, and slice the dice and blackjack tables. They worked steadily for the hour. When it was twenty-eight minutes past eleven o'clock, they stopped until the night watchman made his round, and then waited for Jeff to come and let them out.

The entire operation went off without a hitch.

Nick Coletti was a small, hard-faced individual with dark, deep-set eyes and a thin mustache that did nothing for his appearance. He was a second-generation Sicilian whose father ran an open-air fish market on McDougal Street in Manhattan's Greenwich Village. As a boy, Nick made up his mind that he wanted no part of selling fish, so at sixteen he began running numbers for the Syndicate. He made his first *hit* at nineteen and was given the Hudson assignment when he was only twenty-five. He had remained in control of the small river city for eight years with no worries, difficulties or competition whatsoever.

"Who the hell is doing it?" Nick was yelling at Nappy Gaudio, a thin, wiry hood, and big Bummer Minghini, a giant of a thug; both of whom had grown up with Nick. They, too, were puzzled and frustrated, and had tried every conceivable means of finding out who was harassing them. Even their most reliable sources, the local stool pigeons, were baffled.

Lido Sandrelli, Nick's dandy and dangerous right-hand man, entered the office, smiling. If there was a single reason why Nick maintained his vice-like grip over Hudson, it was tall, vicious Lido Sandrelli. Nick was quite often diplomatic when dealing with the city officials. Big Bummer had a sense of humor and loved children. Nappy Gaudio, a quiet, nervous introvert, would have been completely harmless if he weren't with the others. But Lido, who Marty Politzsky once described as the "Brooklyn Butcher," was the power, the horror, the abject terror behind the throne.

"Just as I thought," Lido boasted. "It's that Mick who owns the pool hall up on Sixth Street."

"Nooo," Nick said.

"I'm telling you it's him."

"I know Charlie O'Brien. He wouldn't think of doing this to me."

"It's him, Nick."

"Not old Charlie. He doesn't have the balls to do something like this. What makes you think it's him?"

"I just got a phone call in my room," Lido explained. "The caller said for us to check the pool hall's desk drawers and we'd find some of the slugs that were used to jam up our slots."

"No," said Nick. "Charlie's not that dumb, and he ain't that ambitious."

"Then let's go check his desk drawers and find out."

"No," Nick said again. "I'll call him." He lifted the phone and found that the lines were dead. Slamming the phone down, he shouted, "Goddammit!"

"Let's go talk to O'Brien, Nick," Lido repeated. "We've got to settle this stuff before we open the new casino in two weeks."

"All right, dammit! Let's go."

A chauffeur was waiting out by the two limousines at the back entrance of the building.

"What have we got?" Nick asked.

"I switched some of the tires around and used a spare," the driver explained. "This one is ready to ride."

"I want the cars locked in the garage every night with an armed guard on them."

"Yes, sir," the chauffeur said as he held the rear door open.

Charlie O'Brien's Pool Parlor was a smoke-filled, two-table joint frequented mostly by the Irish hardhats of Hudson. They were prime targets for the small-town hustlers. Along the left wall was a bar that served good whiskey and draft beer. In one of the back corners sat a poker table and an ongoing five-card-stud game. Today, there were twice as many people watching as there were indulging because a hotshot card player from Brooklyn by the name of Jack Losse had dropped by for some action.

Rotund Charlie O'Brien and young, handsome, slick Jack Losse were the pros at the table and the only winners. More than likely it would have come down to the two of them in a head-to-head freeze-out. But the harsh intrusion of Nick and his hoods soon put an end to that exciting prospect.

Nick and Lido walked directly back to the poker table to confront Charlie as the two henchmen spread out around the pool hall to cover all angles.

Charlie was instantly annoyed and apprehensive. "What is it, Nick?"

"We want to take a look in your desk drawer."

"My desk drawer! What in the hell do—"

Before he could finish his sentence, Lido snatched the older man out of his chair. While being shoved toward the metal desk that sat near the back wall, Charlie stumbled against it.

The customers wanted to help Charlie, but the hoods standing along the walls didn't have their hands in their pockets for self-enjoyment.

Charlie kept looking over at Nick while fumbling through his keys.

"Hurry up," Lido shouted.

When Charlie opened the center drawer, there was only a stack of papers. The first small drawer on the right contained a loaded .45 automatic under a yellow legal pad. But when he opened the second small drawer, the weight surprised Charlie and it fell from his hand and crashed to the floor. "Sweet Mother of God, what the–"

As Charlie stepped back to the wall, Nick reached into his jacket pocket and brought out one of the slugs that had been used to jam his slot machines. He lifted one of the coins from the floor and compared them. They were identical.

"I swear on my mother's grave," Charlie cried, "I don't know how they got there."

"You hid them there!" Lido said and whacked Charlie across the belly with a large blackjack. Charlie doubled up in pain and pleaded with Nick for mercy.

When one of the regulars could stand it no more and decided to try and rescue Charlie, Nick's hoods caught him and pistol-whipped him to the floor.

No one else moved.

Nick Coletti sensed that the slugs were a plant, but he had no choice. "I think it's best you get out of town, Charlie, for your own good."

"I didn't do it, Nick."

"I believe you, Charlie. But I've got to find out who did, and if you're not here, I can't suspect you any more. Can I?"

"I was born and raised here," Charlie whimpered.

"Do you want to die here?" Lido asked as he moved in on him.

"All right, all right, I'll go," Charlie said and sank to the floor.

As Nick turned to leave, he spied Jack Losse at the poker table. Walking over, he asked, "Don't I know you?"

Unruffled, Jack said, "The name's Jack Losse from Flatbush."

"Oh, yeah. You're the poker shark, aren't you?"

"I play a fair game."

"You settling here?"

"Just passing through."

Nick chuckled and said, "Good idea, Flatbush."

As Nick and his men left the pool hall, a small, thin man with a blond crewcut by the name of Tuck Ryan, rushed over to help Charlie to his feet. The old man was crying as he said, "I didn't do anything."

"I know, I know," said Tuck. "But don't worry about it, Charlie. I'll pay you good for this place. Any deal you want, you got it with me."

"But I didn't do anything, Tuck," Charlie repeated.

"I know. I know..."

5

Teddy: "At that point we had to organize. To bring all of the
Hudson teenagers under Junie's leadership. We needed
that much power. At least the strength of an entire com-
bat-ready battalion. Not to use, of course."

In the Center Street office, Junie and Marty were listening to Jeff
Gershon and Donald Morrant arguing whether to use a fuse or an
electronic device. When Jeff said the fuse was more certain to ig-
nite the dynamite, Donald insisted they should trust his ability.
Junie settled the argument by suggesting they hook-up both. If the
device failed, the fuse could be a back-up. "Now, get the hell out of
here!"

As Jeff and Donald were leaving, Tuck Ryan rushed in to an-
nounce that they got O'Brien's Pool Hall. "Nick and those guys
mean business though. They beat the crap out of old Charlie."

Placing his arm around Tuck and taking him aside, Junie said, "If
you want out, I'll understand."

"No," Tuck replied earnestly. "You been good to me. Everybody
else thinks I'm too stupid to work in this stupid town. I'm with you
till the end, Junie, I swear."

"Okay, but forget about chaperoning this place."

While Junie was talking, Teddy entered the room.

"I think it's best that me and you kids not be seen together though until this is over with," Tuck said. "Okay?"

"All right, but I want you to know we're here for you. If they threaten you in any way, you let me know immediately."

"I will, but I'm with you, Junie...till the end. Bye."

After Tuck had departed, Teddy sat, shaking his head while saying, "He's scared."

"I think I'll put some of the older Debs in the pool hall as waitresses to protect him," Junie said. "So how are things going, Marty?"

"Well, Janet Hammond keeps calling and insisting that she's not going to leave us alone until we talk to her."

"All right, we'll go over there. So what's happening, Teddy?"

"I've already talked to the Irish Hawks, the Robinson Street Reds, the Leopards, and the River Rats, and they've all agreed to come in with us. But Johnny Capp, over in Frog Bottom, is giving me a hard time."

"What does he want?"

"Would you believe he wants to fight?"

"Rumble?"

"You got it. Says that's the only way he'll come in...if we beat them."

"What a jerk!" Marty exclaimed.

"All right," Junie sighed. "I've got to make a few phone calls, and I'll talk to that knucklehead to see if I can put some sense into his head."

"Good luck."

Nick Coletti, Lido, Nappy and Big Bummer were sitting in the casino office and trying desperately to figure out who was continuing to harass them.

"How did they get in here?" Nick asked. "Two of the slot machines paid-off and emptied out this afternoon. Fucking bum must of thought he died and went to heaven. We had to shut them all down and check them."

"Maybe we ought to tell the cops," Nappy suggested.

"No cops!" Nick shouted.

"We're going to have to do something, Nick," Lido warned. "I mean with the new casino opening next week and the Don coming all the way up from Brooklyn, we don't need this shit."

"I know, I know," Nick bemoaned.

45

Suddenly there was a triple explosion coming from somewhere in the building. Too startled and frightened at first to move, Nick and the men froze and stared at each other, and then they all ran out into the casino. Seeing smoke coming from the rest rooms, they rushed over just as a man came stumbling out of the smoke and debris.

"What happened?" Nick asked.

"I don't know," the man exclaimed. "I was just sitting there minding my own business and taking a crap when the whole damn room started to blow up. I jumped up, ran into the wall and shit all down my leg. Hell, I'm a mess."

As the smoke began to clear, Nick and Lido stood in the doorway, looking down at the results of the explosions. Three sinks had been blown out of the wall, and the room was flooding as water poured from the fractured pipes. As the maintenance men rushed in with mops and wrenches, Nick and his men turned to go back to the office.

"We gotta bring the cops in on this, Nick," Nappy said as the boss plopped angrily into his chair.

"Maybe they're out-of-towners," Lido ventured.

"No," said Nick. "They're here! And sooner or later they're going to show their faces, and we're going to blow them off."

When the telephone rang, Nick said, "Well, at least *that's* working again. Hello?"

"Do you like what's happening to you?" the muffled voice said over the phone.

"Who is this?"

"Never mind who this is. I asked you a question."

Nick tried to place the voice. "No. No, I don't like it, and you'd better stop if you want to go on living."

"You threatening me?"

"What does it sound like?"

"I was hoping we could get together, talk things over. But I should have known better. You're not that smart. You're greedy."

"What's mine is mine, and nobody takes it from me!"

"We're going to have to see about that."

The Hammond family lived on the suburban northeast well-to-do end of Hudson. It was supposedly the type of neighborhood where kids grew up together and continued to know each other until they died of old age. The house was on the type of street where every morning the paper boy rode a Schwinn bicycle and threw a copy of the *Hudson Star* at the front porch. The milkman wore a white uniform and understood everyone's handwriting; and every house had a back, side and front yard.

All of the fathers were tall, square-jawed, handsome business-men. The mothers were beautiful, loving homemakers. The sons were smart, broad-shouldered and well-mannered. And the girls were all pretty, slim, light-haired and proper.

Janet Hammond was a complete anomaly in her neighborhood. Neither slim nor pretty, she was a large girl with dark hair and eyes and, at sixteen, already more than ten pounds overweight. But none of this mattered at this moment as she sat staring defiantly across the dining table at Junie, Marty, Frank, Butch and Augie while her mother served lemonade.

"Enjoy yourselves," Mrs. Hammond sang before disappearing into the living room where her husband sat reading the evening paper.

"Continue," Marty said quietly to Janet.

"I know what's going on, Marty, and I can help you."

Marty chuckled and said, "What exactly do you think it is we're doing?"

Impatiently, Janet shook her head and said, "Why are we going to waste our time with this garbage?"

"We just wanna' make peace," Augie stated.

"Obviously, there's already peace between you, or you wouldn't be seen together."

"Get to the point, Jan," Junie said.

"All right, I will. You're planning to go against Nick Coletti and take over his operations. Am I right?"

"No," Augie shouted. "You're wrong."

Junie told Augie to be quiet. "Go on, Janet."

Opening a large ledger which also contained a dozen folders, Janet continued, "In this book is a list of every teenager in the city of Hudson. His or her grade point average, aptitude, parents, sib-lings and almost everything else of importance. And I also have a list of certain kids who could be of immediate help to us. For in-stance, Jeff Gershon can open any lock in this town. Donald Morrant is a young genius with electronics, and I've already spoken to him about installing direct, private phone lines between our homes or wherever. He said...it would be easy."

When Frank reached for the ledger, Janet pulled it away. "I just wanted to take a look at it."

"I know what you want, Frank, and you know what I want."

"In other words, you want in."

"You got it, and all the way at a full share of the power."

"Hey, we might need some time to think this over, you know?" said Butch.

"Of course. Take as long as you need...at least until you finish your lemonade."

"We don't need no time to think nothin' ova'," Augie said. "We already know Jeff Gershon can open any lock in town. He's in Center Street."

"What about all the other things?" Janet asked.

"So what. We'll get 'em if we need 'em!"

"There is one other thing," said Janet. "In these folders is the information on the real tyrants of this city. The mayor, the city judge, the police chief and all the others. Some girls are working with me, and we're checking on the city officials every day. Taking secret photos, monitoring who they associate with, and we're even going to start tapping their phones. Sooner or later you're going to have to deal with them, and you'd better have the goods or there goes your plan."

"We'll git it," Augie declared.

Looking directly at Junie Sando, Janet said, "What do you say, Junie?"

"Can't you see what's gonna happin'?" Augie said. "You let her in and she'll wanna bring in her friends, and the next thing you know we got a sewin' circle."

"If I come in, that's it. Let's close it off with what we have right now. If we can't pull this off, no one can."

After a pause, Butch suggested they take a vote.

"What for?" Augie shouted. "We probably woulda' got all that stuff anyway."

"Yes, but she already did."

"So what? We keep bringin' people in, and we're gonna end up with all chiefs and no damn Indians."

"I vote yes."

"Are you crazy, Butch?"

"So do I," Junie stated. "Jan, you're in."

"You guys are nuts!" Augie said. "Let her go be with the Debs where she belongs."

"Sorry, Augie," Janet said. "Oh, yes, before I forget—"

"Here it comes," Augie warned.

"I took it upon myself to rent the old warehouse in Cherry Alley. We can use it as the organization's headquarters. Tomorrow I'll get some people to work on it. I used my own money, and the rent is paid up for two months. By that time I hope we'll be making enough of our own. Okay, what happens now?"

"We're on our way back to Center Street," Frank answered.

"Good. I'll go with you."

As Janet and the boys were going toward the front door, she heard her mother calling from the living room. "Janet, dear, will you come in here a moment please? Your father would like to speak to you."

Janet had a notion of what it would be, so she stepped up to the doorway without entering the room.

Hank Hammond was a gentle, quiet man who had to be prodded by his wife to do almost everything. "Tell her, dear," Katherine Hammond urged him on.

"Well, honey, your mother and I are pleased to see you making friends, but we were wondering if one or two of those boys weren't from...downtown?"

"So what?" Janet asked simply. "I'm not prejudiced, are you?"

"Of course, we aren't, dear," said Katherine. "But proper young ladies are judged by the company they keep. That Augie character looks as if he belongs on a chain gang somewhere. And I don't suppose I have to mention Butch, whatever his name is."

"So just what is it you disapprove of, Mother, your daughter being in their company, the boys being in your home, or the fact that they are not all on chain gangs?"

"Speak to your daughter, dear."

Hank could not find any words to say.

"Thank you, Daddy," Janet said and hurried out the house.

6

Teddy: "Frog Bottom? Are you kidding? In all honesty, the majority of us were more than willing to ignore them and leave them down in the swamps where they belonged. But Junie said he wanted the entire town involved."

Frog Bottom was a dark, gray hamlet that had been built over the swamps south of Hudson. In row after row of weather-beaten, four-room shacks lived men who struggled from morning till night on the lowest-paying, hardest-working jobs in Columbus County. Their women were subservient, dominated, ignorant and prolific. The children were undernourished, somber, shabbily-dressed and following in the perpetual mold. Most of the girls were pregnant by sixteen, forced to quit school and live off their already impoverished families, or marry the teenage father of their child, and then the inglorious cycle would begin again.

The boys of Frog Bottom were all malcontents, bitter, tough, mean and hopeless. As young children their one absurd dream was to become a member of the neighborhood gang that called themselves "The Cavaliers."

At the south edge of the city of Hudson there was a long, cement stairway with no less than fifty steps that dropped into Frog Bottom. Halfway up, someone had been thoughtful enough to build a resting tier with a British lamppost. Waiting there in the night were Junie, Teddy, Marty, Frank and Janet.

The fog cloud covering the hamlet was dense, grayish-black in color and seemed to move in one direction and then the other, bringing with it damp, chilly air.

Gang leader Johnny Capp, a large, lanky, brown-haired, twenty-two-year-old with sharp, cold features, appeared through the fog.

"What do you say, Johnny?" Frank greeted him.

Johnny Capp sneered at Teddy, Marty and Janet.

"Everyone else has agreed to come in with us," Junie began to explain. "All we need is you guys. We've decided to let you in on our plans. We're going to go up against Nick Coletti and run him out of town."

Junie was hoping for a favorable reaction, but Johnny merely stood there, defiantly sucking his teeth.

Finally, he said, "Why am I so important?"

"Because we have to have control and access to the entire city. And to be honest, we need you."

"I know you do," Johnny snickered. "We're the biggest gang in town, so without us you can junk your plans."

"Well, what do you want?" Marty asked.

"Nothin' from you, Hebe."

"Grow up, Johnny!" Janet snapped at him. "What is it?"

"First of all, I don't like no minorities tellin' me what to do, and that's including and especially no little, fat, ugly-ass broads."

"My God," Janet sighed. "I would have hated the Stone Age."

"Isn't there anything we can offer you to make you think it over?" Junie asked.

"Yeah, sure. Put me in charge of the whole damn thing."

"That's ridiculous," said Frank.

"I told you before, Junie, I don't need Center Street. In the last two years, we beat almost every gang in this town except you guys. It's destiny. It's time for us to lock asses."

"But we don't want to fight you, Johnny."

"Tough shit, because there ain't no other way."

When the group fell into a frustrated silence, Johnny sneered at Teddy West and said, "Ain't you got nothin' to say, *bright* boy?"

Softly, Teddy began, "I agree with Junie. I don't want to fight you either, but I can see you're dead set on it. And if it comes to that, we're going to destroy you. We're going to knock you down and kick your brains out while you're lying there."

"You think so, huh?"

"Yes, I do. You're a fool and a masochist, and I guarantee you, you're going to die at a very young age."

Johnny became instantly outraged. "WE OUTNUMBER YOU!" he bellowed out of control. "We outnumber you, two to one."

"It's not enough," Teddy said simply and walked away into the fog. After a moment, he was followed by Frank, Marty and Janet.

As Junie remained facing him, Johnny said, "We've got to lock asses, Junie. There's no other way."

"Yes, there is. Come in with us."

"Our War Counselor is better than Teddy West any day."

"We don't need them, Johnny. You and I are the leaders."

"I wanna rumble," Johnny said plainly.

Speaking softly, Junie began, "I wish I could impress on you how much is at stake here. We don't want to fight you, and we certainly can't afford to lose a rumble right now. And beyond that, you're putting us in a position to make an example of you. Come on, Johnny, grow up."

"We can beat you, Junie."

"Not on your life. Not on your very, very best day. Not if all the powers that be were to fight on your side could Frog Bottom ever defeat Center Street, and you know it. You know it, Johnny."

"You'll see. We'll beat you."

Impatient and frustrated, Junie said, "The only thing you can beat is your meat. And you're probably not even very good at that. You can save us all a lot of grief, Johnny. If you insist on fighting, sooner or later you're going to have to deal personally with me, and I will never show you more mercy than I am right now."

"We'll see."

Junie took a deep breath and said, "Sleep on it, and give me a call at Center Street tomorrow morning at ten."

"I'll call you, but nothin's gonna change."

Johnny turned then and disappeared down the stairs, into the fog and back to Frog Bottom.

Junie made an extra special effort to avert the war with Frog Bottom by waking Kevin Boone, the leader of the Irish Hawks, early the next morning and sending him down to speak with Johnny Capp. Kevin had not reported back, and it was now nearing ten o'clock.

"We must avoid a fight at all cost," Marty Politzsky was saying.

"It's impossible," Teddy exclaimed.

When the wall phone rang, the five teenagers, Junie, Teddy, Marty, Frank and Janet reacted apprehensively.

Junie stood up and answered it after the third ring. "Yes?"

"Hey, it's me, Kevin."

"What did he say?"

"Nothing. They just chased me home. But I can tell you they are preparing for war."

"You all right?"

"I'm fine. Good luck."

Junie hung up the phone, turned to the others and said, "They chased Kevin home."

"Oh, no," Janet groaned. "When we take over, I think we're going to have to keep certain sections of the masses chained to their front porches."

This time when the phone rang, Junie lifted it immediately. "Yes?"

"Time, place and weapons."

"Johnny, we don't want to fight. Let's have another talk. I'm sure we can work something out."

"Time, place and weapons?"

"Johnny..."

"Don't plead with him," Teddy said, angrily.

Junie lowered his head, hesitated a moment more, and then handed the phone to Teddy.

"This is Teddy. What's it to be and where?"

"You name it."

"I'd rather give you the edge, Johnny, you're going to need it."

"We'll see. Name it."

"Okay. Weapons optional, except no guns. Fourth Street playground at noon."

"We'll be there."

Teddy hung up the phone, looked over at Junie, and shrugged. "We've got ourselves a rumble."

"I'll go put out the alarm," Junie said and hurried away.

"Well, Alexander the Great," Janet said to Teddy, "at least you got what you wanted."

"We tried to avoid it, Janet."

"Junie tried to avoid it, you live for it."

"I'm the War Counselor of Center Street, it's my job."

"Calling it your job doesn't make it right!"

53

"Don't you realize what is really important, Teddy?" Marty asked.

"Sure, I do. Center Street. Center Street today, tomorrow, forever. You better get hip to it."

Within moments the Center Street clubhouse began to fill up with members. Mary Granelli and several other Debs, who were in charge of the weapons, were moving the jukebox and lifting the floor boards to get the rubber hoses, chains and other assorted weapons that were hidden there.

All of the members, boys and girls, were donning their war uniforms which consisted of dark blue turtle-neck sweaters and thick leather vests. Some of the boys had metal plates added to their vests, while others had strips of chain mail for added protection.

The big redhead Skippy McDonald, Bruce West, Cat Killer and several other Warriors were standing in a far corner, stripped down to their jock-straps and being "prepared" for physical combat. A few Debs were whipping them with leather straps to temper their bodies for possible hand-to-hand confrontations.

Each member of the Streeters knew exactly what he or she had to do as if they had rehearsed it for hours, which they had under Teddy's adept tutelage.

When Junie returned, Frank Borzak rushed down to him and, speaking in private, said, "We simply can't allow Teddy West to conduct his own little wars. We've got to get rid of him, Junie."

"I don't know how to break this to you, Frank, but Teddy is more important to this thing than you are. Now either you go along with us or get yourself another crew."

Seeing that all fifty members of the Streeters were dressed, armed and ready, Junie walked up in back of the table.

"Et tu, Junie?" Janet said.

"All right!" Junie shouted to get everyone's attention. When the room quieted down and they all turned to him, Junie raised his hands and the members kneeled with their heads bowed in silence as Teddy, Janet, Frank and Marty looked on.

"Let us pray," Junie began the ritual. "Dearest Heavenly Father, we ask not for victory, but only that you will grant us the will and the spirit to do what has to be done. That you will make our opponents worthy of the challenge and keep us all safe from bodily harm. Amen."

"Amen!" the Streeters echoed.

When Janet mentioned to Teddy that she noticed Junie didn't

pray to win, Teddy replied, "You noticed that, did you? That's because they're going to need God's help a hell of a lot more than we are."

"You better not be too sure of yourself, Teddy."

"I'm not sure...I'm positive. We're Center Street."

As the teenagers stood up, Junie shouted, "We will not be denied."

"WE WILL NOT BE DENIED!" the Streeters cried.

"We will not be defeated."

"WE WILL NOT BE DEFEATED!"

"We will be victorious."

"WE WILL BE VICTORIOUS!"

"We are...

"WE ARE...!"

"Center Street."

"CENTER STREET!" they bellowed and began to jump up and down and cheer. "CENTER STREET, CENTER STREET...!"

7

Joseph: "Were you ever concerned about losing?
Teddy: "We certainly should have been, but I don't think we
were. In one of our first rumbles, a kid was hurt, clubbed
badly. Junie took him home and sat up with him all night."
Joseph: "Did that make it okay?"
Teddy: "Of course not. But it was better than doing nothing,
don't you think?"
Joseph: "You seem to have had a hatred for Frog Bottom."
Teddy: "Hate is a pretty strong word. I guess it doesn't matter
now, I can say it. I've out-grown my silly, childish preju-
dices since then. But I *always* looked forward to taking
on those low-class bigoted bastards from down in Frog
Bottom and wiping up the ground with them. Always..."

At 11:35 a.m., the Frog Bottom gang armed themselves and split
up into twos and threes and some larger groups and moved out of
their bleak borough, up the wooded hillside and into the city of
Hudson. Johnny Capp's master plan was to divide into inconspicu-
ous small groups and all join up on the corner of Third Street and
Union Alley and march full-force straight up to the Fourth Street
playground. But Center Street had other plans waiting for them,
hidden in the gangways, abandoned garages and on the lower rooftops, waiting and ready.

As the first three boys from Frog Bottom crossed Fourth Street with their weapons in hand and dashed into a narrow gangway, they were instantly surrounded, jumped and beaten to the ground with lead-filled rubber hoses before they had a chance to defend themselves.

Two blocks away in the parking lot of the five-and-dime store, six more boys from Frog Bottom climbed over a plank-board fence and dropped to the ground only to find themselves facing Streeters who charged into them mercilessly, pummeling and beating them until they were forced to retreat and escape back over the fence.

Attacks and beatings such as these were repeated in alleys and gangways up and down the south side of Hudson as the boys from Center Street formed a gauntlet for five blocks in the middle of the city.

Unaware of the attacks, Johnny Capp and his lieutenants used the safety of the streets to reach the rendezvous point where they waited for the rest of their boys to arrive.

Observing the action through high-powered binoculars on the roof of the Hudson Junior High School at Fourth Street were Junie, Teddy, Mary Granelli and Cindy Wells, a high-ranking Deb.

"What are all you kids doing up there?" the school's janitor shouted as he climbed up on the roof from the fire escape. Barely noticing the janitor, Mary called to Junie who quickly turned and went over to the man.

"You didn't say anything about having all these people up here."

Placing his arm around the janitor's shoulder, Junie guided him away while saying, "Let me talk to you for a moment." Junie said a few things in private, and then the janitor shrugged, nodded and climbed back down the fire escape.

"Something's wrong here, Junie," Teddy announced fearfully.

"What is it?"

"I don't see their Wolf Pack."

"Anybody seen them?" Junie asked.

When the girls said they hadn't, Junie turned to Teddy. "What do you think?"

"My guess is old Johnny Capp has a trick up his sleeve. He sent the Wolf Pack either very far east or to the west, out of the line of our troops. Probably east since he plans to march in from the west."

As Junie and Teddy moved to the east end of the roof, Junie shouted, "Everybody over here."

The girls rushed over and began to search the upper end of town through their binoculars.

"They're out there somewhere," said Junie.

An uneasy silence fell over the four as they stood on the edge of the roof, binoculars locked to their heads. It was a cloudy, overcast day. As a high breeze stirred Mary Granelli's hair, she said softly, "There they are. Crossing the railroad tracks on Fourteenth Street."

"Ahhh yeah," said Junie.

The Wolf Pack was a dozen of the finest and deadliest of the Frog Bottoms. Big, rugged, snarling boys in black leather jackets, chains wrapped around their wrists, straight razors or switchblades in their pockets, blackjacks in their waistbands, and death and destruction in their hearts and minds. They were moving along the railroad tracks that cut through the east end of town. Moving, not in a rush because they had to be cautious not knowing when or where Center Street might attack. But they proceeded in a tight, determined juggernaut primed to react and retaliate on a second's notice.

"They've got to be stopped before they reach the playground," Junie was saying. "And most of our troops are lined up on the south side."

Teddy lifted a walkie-talkie. "Bruce, come in, Bruce. Over."

Bruce West, Teddy's older brother, was moving with his boys through Cherry Alley. "Bruce here. Over."

"How many guys do you have with you?"

"Five. Why?"

"Frog Bottom's Wolf Pack is sneaking in from the east. I want you take what you have and go up to the corner of Fifth Street and Union Alley and wait for them. Over."

"With five guys?"

"I'll send you help as soon as I can. Over and out."

"Call Cat Killer," Junie suggested.

"Cat Killer. Cat Killer, come in. Over."

Down in an abandoned basement, Cat Killer and two other boys, including Augie Sando, had two Frog Bottom soldiers tied to a pole and Cat Killer was whipping them with a hose.

"Cat Killer!" Teddy's voice could barely be heard shouting over the walkie-talkie lying on the floor. Augie lifted it. "Augie Sando here. Over."

"Put Cat Killer on now!" Teddy shouted.

"Cat Killer here, Teddy. Over."

"Where are you? Over."

"We're on Marcum Place."

"Move your people over to Fifth and Union Alley. And run all the way. Over."

"What's up? Over."

"Their Wolf Pack is coming in from the east. They're probably on Tenth Street by now, but we want to attack before they reach Fifth. Bruce will hit them head on and you come in from the south."

"Hell, me and my boys will cut them off before they get there. Over."

"Talk to this asshole, Junie!"

"Cat Killer?"

"Yeah, Junie, I'm here. Over."

"You take your guys and move over to Fifth and Union and meet up with Bruce, or I'm going to kick your ugly ass all over this town. Now move it, over and out!"

When Junie handed the walkie-talkie to Teddy, he began to shout, "Jeff. Jeff Gershon come in. Over."

"I heard it, Teddy. Where do you want us?"

"How many men do you have? Over."

"Seven. Over."

"Okay, Jeff, take as many men as you can gather and move in back of their Wolf Pack. Don't let them see you. When they reach Bruce and Cat Killer, you move in from the rear and hit them hard and fast. Over."

"Got you. We're on our way. Over and out."

Teddy flicked off the walkie-talkie and turned to Junie. "We need somebody to hit them from the north."

Junie knew what he meant. So did Mary, and she was concerned.

"All right. I'll get Butch and a couple of other guys and do it."

Turning to Mary, Junie smiled and said, "Keep your eye on me, baby, and watch my smoke."

As Junie ran to the fire escape, Teddy looked over at Mary and said, "He can take care of himself."

"I know," she said uneasily.

Standing at the end of Union Alley at Third Street, Johnny Capp was now looking around and wondering where his boys were. He checked his watch and it read eleven-fifty-one. Suddenly, one of the soldiers, battered and bloody, came running up to him.

"What the hell happened?" Johnny asked.

"They were waiting for us. Most of the guys were beaten to shit and went running home."

"What?"

Just then two more boys, who had been caught and beat, came running up to Johnny.

"They jumped us," one of them explained. "The rest of the guys ran back home. But we came."

Johnny turned and looked up the alley that would take them to the Fourth Street playground. "If they're using all their men to stop you guys, then the Wolf Pack is safe and should be nearing the playground pretty soon."

"But we don't have enough to go there now!" a lieutenant warned.

"We've got enough. We'll wait until twelve o'clock to see how many more guys come," Johnny said and spat. "Junie Sando, I'm going to kill you."

The Wolf Pack, in Union Alley, was now coming to Sixth Street. Jeff Gershon had picked up five more Streeters and was following the Pack at a safe distance.

Cat Killer had come running up to Bruce West and was told to move up the alley with his boys and hide themselves in a garage in the middle of the block.

Junie grabbed Butch Charles and nine other Streeters. They raced up State Street as fast as they could in an attempt to be on time.

The Wolf Pack was now between Fifth and Sixth Streets in Union Alley when they saw Bruce West and his five guys down at the far end.

The leader of the Pack, Gather Capp, Johnny's brother, held up his hand. The Pack stopped. "They gotta be kiddin'. Them guys against us?"

The Wolf Pack began to move cautiously down the alley and stopped again when they heard someone off in the distance whistle, "Gently Sing the Mocking Birds." Gather knew it was Center Street's theme song and assumed there would be others in the fight besides the boys at the end of the alley.

"Let's go!" Gather yelled. As the Pack started shouting and running toward Fifth Street, Jeff Gershon's group was running up behind them. Half of the Wolf Pack turned to take on Jeff's group while Gather and the other boys continued to run toward Bruce

West. Suddenly, Cat Killer sprang out of the garage to surprise and flank the Wolf Pack before they could prepare. Bruce charged in from the west just as Junie and his guys jumped the fence into the middle of the melee. Instantly, a knife, a six-inch switchblade, came out of the brawl directly at Junie's eyes. He grabbed the wrist, dug his thumbnail so deeply into the flesh and bone that the knife flew from the hand. Junie then sent his elbow crashing into the boy's rib cage, doubling him up and sending him to the ground. But before the kid could land, Junie was faced with two more Wolf Packers, who realizing who he was, went purposefully for him. It was a mistake. Simultaneously, the first one, who was brandishing a black-jack, caught a firm foot in the groin while the other received a karate chop in the throat. Junie then systematically followed up with decisive knockout blows to the jaw and back of the head.

The Frog Bottom Wolf Pack was a formidable group to say the least. Surrounded, outnumbered, outclassed, they put up a coura-geous fight with chains flailing, clubs flying and blades flashing, but there were just too many Streeters. The battle took less than ten minutes, and every member of the Wolf Pack was battered and beaten to the ground. Four boys were seriously injured. Jeff Gershon and Bruce West saw to it that they were taken to the hospital.

Meanwhile, Johnny Capp looked over his small contingent of fourteen reluctant boys and decided to march up to the playground; thinking, of course, his Wolf Pack would meet them there.

When they were halfway up the alley, Junie walked out into the center waving a white handkerchief.

Johnny snickered. "You surrenderin'?"

"It's all over, Johnny."

"We haven't even begun to fight."

Just then Center Streeters began to appear on the rooftops and from behind the fences.

"What's this?" Johnny asked.

"It's all over. You've lost."

A gate opened and Skippy McDonald walked forward with Gather Capp who was bloodied and bowed with his hands tied behind him.

Seeing his brother, Johnny was forced to face the crushing, bitter truth.

Junie walked up to Johnny, extended his hand and said, "Wel-come to Center Street."

Johnny hesitated, looked over at Gather, who had tears streaming down his cheeks, and then glared back at Junie. After frowning a moment more, he finally took Junie's hand.

"Now," Junie said, "now we are one."

In the days that followed, there were a lot of complaints from some parents and a lukewarm investigation by the police. But the code of the streets prevailed. Nothing was said. Not one boy squealed.

8

Teddy: "It was the oddest of places and the weirdest of times to speak of such things. We were passing through the cathouse section of Hudson and returning from the rumble with Frog Bottom when Junie said, 'The family is all important, Teddy. And now that we are one, God knows that's what we have to become, a loving, caring family.' When I asked what God had to do with it, he said everything. I told him it couldn't be because it takes away our free will. 'More importantly, the share of meager glory that belongs to us.' Junie simply stared at me, shook his head and said, 'Don't try to philosophize, Teddy. You're not very good at it. Your job, your one purpose in life, is to see that Center Street wins, wins everything. If we ever lose, the blame is going to fall directly on you. So I would suggest you keep your mind on that and nothing else. Besides that...sometimes you're full of shit.' He then smiled and walked away."

The St. Mary's 10:00 a.m. Sunday Mass was being conducted by an elderly priest accompanied by a handsome, young altar boy on each side.

The 10:00 a.m. meeting at the Center Street clubhouse was being conducted by Frank Borzak with Skippy McDonald on one side and Bruce West on the other.

The altar boys were holding their hands across their chests as the priest kissed the relic saint.

Skippy and Bruce were holding clubs as Frank briefed all of the gang leaders on the major plan.

The Catholic priest began, "*In the name of the Father, and of the Son and of the Holy Spirit.*"

"*Amen,*" the congregation responded.

Frank Borzak began, "Junie Sando asked me to bring you here this morning so I could brief you on what we're about to do. On pain of severe punishment, you are all now sworn to secrecy, or you have the choice of leaving this room right this minute."

The gang leaders had waited long enough to find out what was going on. No one moved. Present were Kevin Boone of the Hawks, Dominic Gambino of the Rats, Louis MacKey of the Black Leopards, Johnny Capp of Frog Bottom, and Boris Robanski of the Robinson Street Reds.

"Where's Junie Sando?" Kevin asked.

"He's at Mass."

"*The grace of our Lord Jesus Christ and the love of God and the fellowship of the Holy Spirit be with you all.*"

"*And also with you.*"

"Now, I know some of you probably already know what we're doing," Frank continued. "But since your services are going to be invaluable starting now, we've decided to have this briefing. We are going to take over Nick Coletti's operations. We've already started to harass them, and tonight we're going to sabotage the opening of Nick's new casino. Gentlemen...we are at war."

"*The Grace and Peace of God our Father and the Lord Jesus Christ be with you.*"

"*Blessed be God, the Father of our Lord, Jesus Christ.*"

"Each one of your sections will be assigned to protect a member of the board day and night. And you will be held personally responsible for anything that happens to them, on pain of severe punishment. Also, each one of you leaders will be responsible for a member of the Mob. If they decide to strike back at us in any way, you will eliminate your assignment in the style to which they have grown accustomed. And last, but not least, you will keep tight controls and run your sections with an iron fist. You will be responsible for any and all of your members who screw-up. And believe me, the punishment will be severe. Are there any questions?"

The room remained silent.

The congregation at the Catholic Mass had lowered their heads, but Junie Sando, standing next to Mary Granelli, could feel eyes upon him. He turned left and saw Tuck Ryan with his head bowed, but leaning so he could look past his wife.

Junie looked and saw little thirteen-year-old Tony Coletti standing next to Nick but with his head turned and smiling back at Junie. When Junie smiled and winked, the kid returned to the front. But standing on the other side of Tony was Lido, and he was staring back at Junie with a cold, skeptical glare. Junie merely smiled, nodded slightly and lowered his head. Lido did likewise when Nick whacked him on the arm.

"*The Lord be with you.*"

"*And also with you.*"

Frank Borzak pulled five envelopes out of the drawer and placed them on the desk. "In each of these envelopes is a large sum of money and a note with your personal instructions. You will read it, memorize it, destroy it and follow it to the letter. Are there any questions?"

When everyone remained silent, Frank told the leaders to come forward. As the boys walked up to the desk, Louis MacKey of the Leopards took his envelope and asked, "Just how many of us is supposed to be alive when this shit is done with?"

Frank shrugged and said, "Enough."

The law firm of Brink and Pugh was far less than prestigious even for a small city like Hudson. Stanley and George, respectively, could cause anyone to wonder about the degree of difficulty of the New York State Bar exam, as well as the integrity of the Bar Association. They were a sleazy twosome, to say the least: fat, sloppily dressed, hairy, constantly smoking cigars as well as burping and breaking wind out loud. Their most recent case was a text book example of a miscarriage of justice. They defended a husband who was found not guilty of abusing his wife even though the battered woman had lost five teeth and was left deaf in one ear. The husband, through Brink and Pugh, was now counter-suing the woman for defamation of character.

They weren't usually open for business on Sunday afternoons, but a telephone call from Tuck Ryan had awakened George Pugh at one o'clock in the morning. "If you're interested in making half-a-million dollars tax-free, be at your office with Stanley at two o'clock this afternoon."

Needless to say, the greedy attorneys were surprised to see Janet Hammond, Marty Politzsky and four teenage toughs enter the small, modest office. The lawyers shrugged at each other as two of the Warriors placed chairs in front of the desk for Janet and Marty.

Running late, Tuck Ryan rushed into the office and apologized. "Sorry, I had to go home and change clothes. I wore my suit to Mass."

"What's this all about, Tuck?"

"Ahh, the, ah...Janet and Marty will explain it to you guys."

Turning suspiciously to the teenagers, George Pugh said, "Well?"

Janet nodded for Marty to begin.

"Who do you think is the most corrupt public official in Hudson?"

"Take your pick," George said and laughed.

"You're right," said Marty. "And not only are most of them on the take, but a few have even invested with Nick Coletti."

"How do you know that?" George Pugh asked, continuing to speak for the two lawyers as both of their interests were suddenly aroused.

"Never mind how we know it," said Janet. "Go on, Marty."

"To get right to the point, gentlemen, it doesn't really matter who's running this corrupt little town of ours as long as we all keep cashing in. Right?"

The lawyers were silent, wondering to themselves just what Marty had in mind. George took a moment, and then defiantly said, "Yes, I think it does matter who runs this town."

"Do you like the way Nick is running it?"

"Who says he is?"

"Don't crack wise with us, George," said Janet. "We don't have time for it."

George glared at Janet as one of the soldiers from the Black Leopards leaned in on him. George turned to the large, mean-looking kid and then shouted, "All right, all right, what do you want?"

"It has been brought to our attention," Marty continued, "that Nick Coletti and his entire contingent will be leaving our fair city very shortly, and we were wondering if we could count on your technical assistance."

"To do what?"

"To do whatever we want you to do," Janet snapped.

Marty chuckled as the lawyers once again glared at Janet.

"We're all Hudsonians here," said Marty. "There's no reason why we can't work together on this thing and all profit greatly from it."

"I think what the kids are trying to say to you guys," Tuck explained, "is that if we all work together, we'll all get something out of it."

After a pause, George asked, "How are you going to do it?"

"We'll show you and tell you," said Marty, "but first we have to know where you stand."

George looked at Stanley, and the quiet lawyer nodded.

"Okay, we're in," said George.

"You'd better mean it," Janet warned them.

George was beginning to hate Janet. "We keep our word."

"I believe them," Marty said as he lifted a folder from his briefcase and tossed it across the table.

Opening the folder, George couldn't believe what he saw. There were photos of the chief of police visiting one of the brothels, another picture of the mayor lunching with Nick Coletti, and shots of the casinos inside and out. There was also a tape.

"What's on this?" George asked.

"Something the mayor would not want heard by anyone."

"All right," George said, "so you got some stuff. This still doesn't get rid of Nick Coletti. You're not going to scare him with pictures and tapes."

"Let us worry about Nick," Janet said. "We're offering you one heck of a deal, and you know it."

"But at what price?"

"We're willing to trust you completely," said Marty. "So much so, that we're going to turn all of this information over to you. You'll have this and more. And from time to time we might call upon you for a favor or two."

"Where does our cut come in?"

"We'll take care of you, George, big time," Marty said and handed the lawyer the folders.

George began to leaf through the material.

Tuck Ryan thanked the attorneys as he left the office. The Warriors followed him out as Janet and Marty walked to the door.

"This is a sad joke. You know that, don't you?" George asked.

"Nick Coletti, and especially Lido, are going to destroy you brats."

"We're not concerned," Marty said.

"Who's going to save you, who's going to protect you?"

"Like I said, we're not concerned, and you shouldn't be either."

"You're taking one hell of a chance leaving this stuff with us, aren't you?" George asked. "I mean without this, there goes your whole ball game. If I wanted to, I could go straight to Nick and make my own deal, and you punks would be screwed."

Marty and Janet looked at each other. Then Marty said, "You had to say it, didn't you? You couldn't just take it for granted that we had all the bases covered, could you?"

"What are you talking about?"

"Moe!" Janet called.

Moe Garnett, the Black Leopard, came back into the office with a definite purpose. George and Stanley sat up apprehensively, not knowing what to expect.

"Tell them," Janet said to Moe who stood at least six-foot-one with arms like Goodrich tires and decorated with scars and burns from countless street battles. At first he smiled, then looking directly at George, Moe said, "George Pugh, you live at 954 State Street. You have three kids: Sheila, Betty and Bucky. Your wife's name is Margaret, and she weighs one-hundred and twelve pounds. There is a crack in the lower right-hand corner of the big bay window in your living room."

George was stunned.

"Stanley Brink, you live at 315 Crestview Drive, and you have two kids: Linda and Greg. Your wife's name is Jean, and she weighs one-hundred-thirty. And...the upper left-hand hinge on your back screen door is coming loose."

Suddenly, Stanley was on his feet and yelling, "You stay away from my family, you black bastard!"

Moe merely chuckled as he backed out of the office.

"Charming. Very, very charming, Stanley," said Janet. "Are there any other pleasantries you care to express?"

Stanley sank into his chair.

"Everything is going to be just fine, gentlemen," Marty assured them.

"Yes, just fine," Janet added. "As long as you do exactly what you're told."

After the teenagers were gone, George and Stanley sat quietly pondering their dilemma. There was no one to call; no one to help them. They could warn the others, but they were selfish men.

"What are we going to do, George?" Stanley finally uttered.

After a pause, George answered, "I don't think we have a choice, Stan. Do we?

"Oh, my Lord."

"Let's don't circle the wagons yet. This doesn't necessarily have to be a bad thing. Some good can come out of anything, not to mention a healthy profit."

"I can't believe you're saying this, George. That... That *boy* threatened my family."

"It wasn't exactly a threat, Stan. It was more like a warning. I think we can easily stay in the background in this thing."

"I'm not staying anywhere," Stanley stated. "Not even in this town."

9

Teddy: "God, we loved it. I can't tell you how much we loved
it. Even when we received the news that the Don was
coming to Hudson, you would have thought it was someone as innocuous and docile as Santa Claus the way Center Street reacted. Frank Borzak, of course, suggested we
assassinate the Don and put an immediate end to the entire situation, or begin the war in earnest. No one agreed
with him, which wasn't unusual. We all wanted the challenge. That's how certain we were of ourselves, how con-
fident, yes, and...how utterly childish and foolish."

The late afternoon sun began to cool and prepare for the night as
long, dense shadows found their way across the streets and lawns
of the city. Traffic was sparse; and from the top of the Columbus
County Hospital, the county's tallest building, the two boys could
see everything that moved.

"You know what I heard?" Augie was saying to Butch. "That your
momma eats dingleberries and sour cream for breakfast."

"Is that right? Well, I heard your momma's just like the transcon-
tinental railroad. She's been laid all over the country."

The two boys laughed as Augie walked a few yards away and
began to relieve himself on the roof of the hospital.

"Knock that off!" Marty Politzsky yelled while crossing the roof.

"See anything yet, Butch?"

"No, and we ain't gonna'," Augie said while buttoning his fly and coming back over to them.

"Why not?"

"Because they're coming by train."

"Junie doesn't think so."

"So, my brother don't know everything."

"It doesn't matter," said Butch. "'cause we got the station covered, too."

"Hey, Marty, is it true that the warehouse is ready?" Augie asked.

"Yes. Janet has it all cleaned up, and it's looking real sharp. That will be our headquarters from now on."

"What's that?" Butch shouted and pointed down to a line of four black cars coming along highway 9H that entered Hudson from the southeast.

"It's a funeral," Augie exclaimed.

"Funeral nothing," said Marty. "It's them!"

Butch Charles was instantly on the walkie-talkie. "Cornbread, Cornbread, can you hear me? Over."

"Roger, Bakey Bean. What have you got? Over."

"Four, black limousines on 9H heading right for Diamond Street. Pony Express has arrived. Over and out."

"Let's go!" Marty shouted.

The Don, Mario G. Carlucci, was an extremely handsome man of fifty-five with Latin features, a pleasant smile and bright, intelligent eyes. He was sitting alone in the back seat of the third limo with his personal chauffeur driving and his deadly bodyguard, Angelo Russo, also sitting in the front seat.

"Nick's got a pretty good assignment here," Russo remarked. "Clean air, plenty of space, fresh apples."

The Don chuckled and said, "Think we should switch places with him?"

Russo and the chauffeur laughed as the caravan crossed Tenth Street, moving along the park. Suddenly a teenage boy riding a bicycle came directly into the path of the first car. The driver screeched to a halt, but too late. The boy tumbled onto the front of the car and somersaulted against the windshield as the bike was crushed and dragged. The following cars all slid to a halt, barely avoiding a pile-up.

Instantly the bodyguards, henchmen, and even the Don's attorney, were out of the cars. They helped to create a bizarre crowd of people which included the plainly dressed Hudsonians, a large, instant group of teenagers, the curious country folks, and this sudden intrusion of deadly serious men dressed in dark summer suits.

The driver of the first car hurried to see if the boy was hurt. The teenager climbed down from the car while holding his head and appearing faint.

"Why didn't you watch where you were going?" Janet Hammond asked the driver as she appeared out of the crowd. She was echoed by several other teenagers.

"He came out of nowhere," the driver exclaimed.

"Sure, that's what they all say."

As a couple of the hoods moved angrily toward Janet, Moe Garnett and Skippy McDonald appeared out of the crowd and stood beside her.

"What seems to be the problem here?" the Don's smooth attorney came forward and asked.

Janet moved over to the bike rider who was being held up by the driver and one of the henchmen. "I'll take care of him," she said and took the boy's arm, guiding him away. "They don't care about you. They don't care about us. We're just a bunch of hicks as far as they're concerned."

The attorney moved nonchalantly over to the boy, slipped him a fold of bills and said, "You're okay now, aren't you? Just a bump, right?"

Feeling the money securely in his hand, the kid began to smile and move around while testing his neck and head. "I'm fine. Just a little tumble. I'm okay."

"Are you sure?" Janet asked.

"I'm positive. Let's go."

The teenagers began to disappear as quickly as they had formed.

Having seen it all, Don Carlucci rested back in his seat with a cynical smile on his face. He was anything but at ease at that moment.

Janet and several of the teenage boys had turned the corner on Ninth Street when Butch Charles and Augie Sando caught up to them.

Butch said, "You should have seen the look on the Don's face."

"He was shittin' a brick!" Augie shouted.

"They're going to drop a lot of bricks before we're through with them," Janet said. "This is *our* city, and we're going to let everybody know it."

"Gee, we're really bad. I mean *bad*!" Butch said and laughed.

The new casino, simply called "The Apache," was a two-story wooden structure just north of Second Street on Diamond with a huge parking lot fronting it and a thick line of oak trees hiding the building.

Nick Coletti had received word from New York that the opening was to be a small, intimate affair with a select few including well-known regulars, a few local VIPs and any politician with the nerve to be seen. Many of the people invited were debating even in this final hour, whether or not to attend. Not so of Mr. and Mrs. William Charles. They were dressed like "*Sunday*," and Butch's mother was all smiles when he came running into the house. "Hey, Ma, you look pretty. Where you guys goin'?"

"Your daddy's been invited by Mr. Coletti to the new casino openin'."

Butch was stopped. "Why would he invite Daddy?"

"You know your daddy's been workin' down there at night."

"As a janitor! Why would they invite a janitor?"

"Your daddy happens to be a maintenance man."

"He's a janitor, Ma! That's all he is, is a damn janitor!"

"You watch your mouth, boy, or I'll slap the daylights outta you!"

"I'm sorry, Momma, but I heard there's gonna be some trouble down there tonight."

"They been havin' all kinds of trouble, but nothin' your daddy ain't been able to fix," Emma Charles said proudly. "That's probably why Mr. Coletti invited us. He's pleased with what your daddy's been doin'."

"Hah," said Butch. "He probably invited you 'cause he couldn't get nobody else to come."

"What are you talkin' about, Butchie Lee? There's gonna be a crowd of peoples there tonight."

"Not for long," said Butch. "Momma, take my word for it, you ain't gonna have a good time there tonight. It's gonna be awful in there."

Emma Charles knew the honesty of her son. As she glared at him, she asked, "What you know, Butchie Lee?"

"I know you shouldn't go there tonight, and that's all I know."

"Who told you somethin' was happ'nin' there tonight?"

"The word's all over town."

"Maybe your daddy should call and tell Mr. Coletti about it."

"Momma...do you want your little baby boy here to be on Mr. Coletti's bad list? You have Daddy call him, and he gonna ask how he knows and Daddy's gonna say, 'Well, my son said so and so.' Now, if nothin' happens there tonight, you have my permission to beat the daylights outta' me in the morning. I will gladly lay my little hiney down across the chair and let you whip me to death if nothin' happens there tonight. Please, Momma, please don't go."

"What'll I tell your daddy?"

"Tell him you don't feel too good. You got the worse headache you ever had in your entire life. Tell him anything that'll work, but don't go."

"Where you been, boy?" big Bill Charles said, coming into the living room while tying his tie. "I done told you a hundred times I don't want you goin' out into that street until your bed is made and your room is spotless. Now, your mother done told me that you cain't hear too good. Now I ain't holdin' down no two jobs for you to be runnin' the streets like some damn hoodlum. Do you understand?"

"I'm sorry, Daddy, but I had something important to do."

"I don't care what you think is important. I want that bed made and that room clean!"

"Yes, Daddy. It won't happen again."

"It betta' not."

"Excuse me," Butch said and rushed away.

When he reached the top of the stairs, his sister Jeri-Mae, seventeen, was coming down the hall while pulling on her windbreaker.

"Where you goin'?" Butch asked.

"I've been assigned to the night shift at O'Brien's Pool Hall."

"What? You, Miss Straight-A Prima Donna, who's been saying all these years you wouldn't wait no tables for nobody?"

"I'm not doing it for just *anybody*, am I, birdbrain? And I'm not there just to wait tables, either, am I, dorkhead?"

"Birdbrain, dorkhead," Butch mocked her as Jeri-Mae ignored him and went downstairs.

Nick Coletti had his two top men, Lido and Nappy, on the front door of the casino. They were perusing everyone closely. When

Tuck Ryan and his wife entered, they searched him and checked his wife's purse.

"Have a nice time," Nappy said as the Ryans melted into the crowd. People were at the slot machines and both dice tables were fully active as were the ten blackjack tables.

In the dining area Nick had set up a roped-off section for Don Carlucci and his party. Nick's wife, Sally Coletti, a handsome, dark-eyed woman, looked at the Don and said, "What do you think, Mario?"

The Don merely smiled, took Sally's hand and nodded as he watched the crowd.

Nick's son, little Tony Coletti, had gone to the men's room three times and nothing had happened. This time he really had to relieve himself. As he stood at the tub-style urinal, a man stood next to him, unzipped his fly and said, "*Gently sing the mocking birds.*"

"What?"

"I said *Gently sing the mocking birds.*"

"Oh, right. *As they're passing by.*" Tony finally answered and then took a small box out of his pocket and handed it to Tuck Ryan, who shook his head impatiently and left the restroom.

The first person to notice the foul odor was a cocktail waitress, who immediately reported it to Lido. He, in turn, excused himself from the private party, went to the air conditioner, got a good whiff of the pungent, sickening smell and immediately shut it down.

Seeing Bill Charles at the blackjack table, Lido called to him.

"Oh, hi, Mr. Sandrelli. Thanks for invitin' us, but my wife took sick and couldn't–"

"To hell with that," said Lido. "What's wrong with the damn air conditioner?"

"What's that stink?" Bill asked, suddenly aware of the odor.

"I don't know, but you'd better find out."

Lido looked over at the private party and saw that the Don had already risen to leave. They managed to escape without being noticed.

Soon the entire room was filled with the musty odor. One rather large lady, standing at the slot machines, started coughing and ultimately fainted.

Nick came running over to Lido. "What is it!?"

"Something in the air conditioner. Bill Charles is looking at it now."

As more and more customers were becoming ill from the repugnant smell, many were rushing toward the doors. Nick stood up on a chair and raised his hands as he shouted, "Everything is all right, folks, just a little trouble with the air conditioning. That smell is just some harmless...ah, gas. It won't hurt you at all. It'll be fixed in just a moment."

Lido and the other henchmen were rushing to open all the doors and windows.

There was a die-hard dice shooter with a hot roll going who didn't even smell the odor, much less have any intention of ducking out of the nearest exit.

When Nick and Lido got back to the air conditioner, Bill Charles had dug the tiny, powerful stink pellet out of the fan unit and was running with it into the alley.

During the confusion, Tuck Ryan had worked his way over to the heating system, turned the thermostat up to its maximum and then left the casino with his wife.

As Nick rushed back inside to try once again to calm everyone, Bummer told him there was a phone call in the office.

"Hello!" Nick yelled into the phone, only to hear someone laugh at him and hang up. Nick slammed the phone down as an incomprehensible anger and frustration gutted him. He stood there shaking in the throes of agony and bitterness until Bummer came into the room. "You all right, boss?"

Coming out of his spectral trance, Nick awoke and said, "Yes, I'm okay. Where did Mario and the others go?"

"Sally invited them to your house for drinks."

"Good," Nick sighed in relief. "Damn, it's hot in here. Is it just me?"

"No, it's hot," Bummer agreed.

Going over to the vent, Nick felt the waves of hot air being blown into the room, and screamed, "Goddammit! Who put the fucking heat on?"

As Nick's voice echoed through the casino, it was followed by a shattering explosion that destroyed the heating system and sent flames cascading across the ceiling that turned on the sprinklers. As the water rained down throughout the building, the remaining customers and all the workers ran for the nearest exits. Even the die-hard dice shooter, though reluctantly, had to finally discontinue his hot roll.

Less than an hour later the casino was empty except for the workers attempting to clean up the mess. Nick Coletti was sitting in his office and glaring at the telephone on the desk. Lido, Nappy and Bummer were with him. Nappy spoke first to break the silence. "Maybe they won't call to-"

"They'll call!" Nick snapped at him.

All of the men reacted when the phone finally rang.

"Yes?"

"Hi!"

"Whoever you are, you're going to die!" Nick raged into the phone.

"My God, man, haven't you had enough? I was hoping you were ready to talk. That we could set up a meeting for Tuesday morning."

Nick found himself saying, "Where and what time?" before he realized what he had done.

"That's better. We'll call you Tuesday morning at ten o'clock and tell you where to come. Everything is going to be just fine from now on, Nick. No more harassments, and you'll be back in charge. Oh, by the way, have a thousand dollars handy on Tuesday. Are there any questions?"

"No."

"And, Nick...don't do anything you'll regret."

10

Teddy: "Death? Are you kidding? We were too young and too naive to be that realistic. First of all, we were convinced that Nick wouldn't dare harm us simply because we were quote-unquote 'children.' And, second of all, if they touched us, we would strike back at them unmercifully. I think we wanted to convince them of that. Not that we ever actually intended..."

The hour was late, the crowd quiet, the mood was uneasy, yet Sally Coletti was smiling as she served coffee to the men and then politely retreated to another part of the house. Nick was so embarrassed and flustered by what had happened that he sat with his face in his hands. Don Carlucci, relaxed as always, was listening patiently to each man's speculation.

"I think it's outsiders," Nappy was contending.

"What outsiders? From where?" Russo shouted.

"I don't know yet. Maybe it's the Manhattan Barbuta mob."

"They wouldn't try it," said Bummer.

"I think it's a couple of guys right here in town," said Lido. "Maybe some of them Atlas cement workers trying to get a couple of extra bucks. When we catch them, they're going to be wearing some of that cement."

"Hey," Nappy said, coming up with a completely different idea.

"Maybe it's the cops. They figure we can't touch them."

Nick looked up. "You know, he might have something there. What do you think, Mario?"

The Don looked at each man, smiled and then said softly, "You're all wrong. I knew who it was the minute we came into town."

"Who is it?" Nick asked impatiently.

"You should have figured it out, Nick. You should have figured it out and cut it off before it got out of hand."

"Who is it, Don Carlucci?" said Lido. "We can take care of it, believe me."

Mario chuckled and said, "Don't any of you have the slightest idea?"

"Is it the cops?" Nick asked.

Mario looked at the men again and said simply, "It's the teenagers."

"The teenagers!?" they all exclaimed in unison.

Pointing at Nick, Mario said, "You check on that boy who was hit by the limousine this afternoon, and I'll give you ten to one he's on the high school tumbling team. And that girl who was doing all the talking, I'll give you the same odds she's one of the leaders."

"I'll break those punks in two," Lido snarled.

"You think so, huh?" said Mario. "When she was talking, two of the meanest looking boys I have ever seen anywhere were standing there to protect her."

"If it's that little ugly broad, I'll-"

"No, no, Lido." Mario frowned. "You're not thinking. The person who organized them wouldn't be out in the streets. Out in the open where we could see him. He's got them together into a precise, working machine with one unique purpose...to get rid of the big bad wolves. They hate you here, Nick. They hate us almost everywhere. We've always known that, so we've demanded respect, and we made sure they were afraid of us. But these...kids aren't afraid of anything or anybody."

"They will be if we knock off two or three of them," said Lido.

"That might have worked in the beginning," Mario chuckled, "but now I'm afraid you've waited too long and given them too much time and confidence."

"Suppose we find out who the leader is and get rid of him?" Nick asked.

"That might work, but I'd be willing to bet that'll be the best kept secret in this town. And then again, there might be a back-up who will be as powerful, and maybe even more dangerous and deadly. Number-two men usually are," Mario said and looked over at Lido. "Let me speak with Nick alone."

The other seven men, with the exception of Russo, who never left Mario's side, all bowed to the Don as they departed.

"I'm sorry, Mario," Nick said and lowered his head.

Reaching over and grasping Nick by the back of his neck, Mario caressed and shook him. "Hey, it's okay. You've done a fine job here until now. Your payments are good and always on time."

"I just should have figured it out. You're so smart, you got it right away. I just want to do good by you, Mario."

"Nick," Russo spoke up, "you're my brother-in-law. Believe me, we're not going to let anything happen to you. But you gotta straighten this out."

Nick stared at Russo and knew that the hit man could easily say those words one minute with God as a witness, and then, if given the order, kill him the next second without a thought or hesitation.

Nick turned to Mario and stuttered, "The, ah, the, ah, payments. This month's payment is almost ready to go. Nappy and Bummer will drive it down...as usual."

"You see," said Mario. "Everything is just fine. Now, do you have any idea how to handle these kids?"

"Well, to be honest with you I'm meeting with them on Tuesday morning. They called tonight after the... I told them I would meet with them. They said the harassments would be over with. That I'd be in charge again."

Mario and Russo looked at each other.

"Not that I ever lost control." Nick chuckled nervously. "But they will definitely stop what they're doing."

Mario leaned back in his chair to give it some thought. "Maybe I should send you some help."

"I can handle it. It'll all be over after I talk to them on Tuesday. I swear to you, Mario."

Mario stood. "I guess we'd better start back."

"I want you to trust me, Mario. Have confidence in me that I can still do the job here," Nick said as they walked to the door.

Patting Nick on the cheek, Mario said again, "I think I'll send you some help."

As Mario and Russo came outside, Lido, Nappy and Bummer went back into the house.

Sally Coletti entered the living room just as Nick and his men were taking seats. "Can I get you something?"

The men didn't want anything.

As Sally went to the kitchen, Lido said, "I don't think the Don is too happy about what's happening here, Nick."

"I'm not happy about it either!"

Little Tony Coletti, who had been hiding in the darkness at the top of the stairs, was beginning to doze off. Certain that everything of importance had already been said, he got up and went to his bedroom.

There were several late night meetings between Junie Sando and George Pugh, and quite often they would take place at a little, greasy spoon called Bell's Pond Diner that rested at the desolate and lonesome crossroads of routes 9 and 9H. The stainless steel eatery was nine miles directly east of the city.

Late supping with Junie and George were Johnny Capp, Skippy McDonald, Moe Garnett and Kevin Boone. They had all feasted on double cheeseburgers, french fries with gravy, egg creams, and were topping it off with hot apple pie à la mode when the lawyer said, "Here comes your biggest problem."

All of the boys expected to look up and see Lido Sandrelli. But instead, stepping from their car were two, tall New York State Troopers dressed in their flat-gray uniforms with purple ties and cowboy hats. They were wearing large .38 caliber revolvers on the hip and both appeared to be humorless men with piercing blue eyes and granite jaws. Walking directly forward after entering the diner, they took seats at the formica-topped counter. One looked around the room and, seeing the crowd in the corner, whispered something to the other. They both glared at the group for a moment and then turned to an old, late-shift waitress who was pouring their coffees.

"We can take 'em," Skippy chuckled.

"Fuckin' A," said Johnny. "One-on-one we'd have 'em begging for mercy. Right, Moe?"

Moe and Kevin, being more realistic, merely smiled at the thought.

"They'd have to call out the National Guard to take us on," Skippy added. The four boys laughed.

After a pause, Junie said, "Some day they'll come. They will come, but they won't be able to touch any of us because some of us will be...absent, and the rest will be immune."

Everyone stared at Junie while trying to fathom what he meant. The word "absent" stuck with each of them. Kevin wanted to know why the State Police would even bother with Hudson.

"Sooner or later," said Junie, "all corrupt towns are cleaned up. And those are the guys who do it."

Johnny turned again to look at the Troopers, snickered and said, "Let 'em come."

11

Joseph: "I find it hard to believe that so many people went along with it."

Teddy: "Come on, realize the situation for what it was. We're talking small, square town here."

Joseph: "But it all seemed so fragile, so precarious, as if one person could have tipped the scales against you."

Teddy: "Would you have wanted to be that person? Try to fathom what it must have been like for the outsiders."

Joseph: "I wouldn't have taken part."

Teddy: "Don't kid yourself. We all crave security and immortality. You would have joined, Sherm."

Joseph: "I know myself, Teddy. So, everybody stuck with you?"

Teddy: "At that time they did. We had to kick one kid out. Cat Killer. He was great in the beginning, but then he started to go buggy. He lived alone with his alcoholic father who used to beat him until we found out about it and tied his father to a tree and hosed him down. He never touched Cat Killer again."

The sun was shining high and bright that Monday morning. So much so that Junie Sando was shading his eyes while sitting on the fender of his Studebaker at the mouth of State Alley. Boris Robanski and Skippy McDonald were warning him that he would have to clean house.

"He's dangerous," Boris stated. "Sooner or later he's going to do something really crazy. We're too close to have to worry about him."

"He stays pretty much to himself, doesn't he?"

"That's not the point, Junie. He's wearing Center Street colors every day."

Junie frowned his frustration as Skippy added, "We know he was one of your original members, but it's different now. And when you see him, you'll see why."

Skippy led the way as the three boys entered State Alley, passed a garage and then crossed a deserted lot strewn with rusty tin cans, car parts and some butterfly weed. On the other side of the lot was a high, sturdy, makeshift fence built of uneven and discolored boards with a door gate in the center.

"Hey, Cat Killer! Cat Killer, you in there?" skippy called to him.

"No, I'm not," came the unfriendly reply.

"Open up, we want to talk to you."

"Junie Sando, is that you?"

"Yes, it's him," Boris yelled. "Now open up."

The three boys waited impatiently while listening to the sounds of three bolt locks being opened on the door gate. As the boys entered the yard, Junie was appalled by what he saw, an obviously disturbed nineteen-year-old boy wearing a Mohawk haircut, war paint and a filthy, blue turtleneck sweater with a tattered leather vest.

"Welcome."

The dirt yard had everything from a couple of broken sofas, a steel rack filled with discarded clothes, broken bottles, empty cat food cans, and more than a dozen old tires. When Boris tapped Junie's arm, the three boys looked at something more than repulsive. A gray alley cat freshly impaled on the top of a six-foot pole. At the base was a wooden sign that read: "Cat of the day."

"What's that?" Junie asked.

"One of them flea-ridden cats. Those damn things are taking over the city. People have a litter and then let them run loose. They're disease carriers, Junie. I get rid of as many as I can."

Junie looked around the yard and noticed the rotting pile of beheaded cats in a far corner. Coming back to Cat Killer, he said, "Is there a rumble I don't know about?"

"Oh," Cat giggled and touched his vest. "No, I just want to be ready when you call me. I'm always ready."

Junie gazed around the yard again, frowned and said, "Take it off."

"What?"

"You heard him!" Skippy shouted.

"But it's mine! I bought this."

"They're Center Street colors, and we don't wear them every day," Junie said calmly.

Boris Robanski took a mean step toward Cat.

"I demand a hearing!" Cat shouted as he began to unbutton his vest. "You don't have the right to come here and disband me. Dismiss me. Dismantle me. You don't have the right." He ripped off the last button and snatched off the vest and threw it to the ground. "These...these two animals, you heathens you have nothing to say to me, about me. We kicked their asses and they don't have the right to come here and dismiss me." He was groveling now as he pulled the sweater off and threw it at Junie's feet. Hugging the naked top half of his body, Cat Killer was shuddering, not from the air, it was 80 degrees, but from hate. "I swear in the sight of almighty God, you will regret this." Turning to Skippy and Boris, he added, "You heathens are nothing! I demand a hearing from my peers. I want to talk to Teddy West. I bet he's not part of this. I was a good soldier, Junie. A damn good soldier." Cat Killer shrank to the ground as Skippy picked up the vest and sweater. He and Boris left the yard. Junie stood there while Cat remained on his knees, cowering and covering himself. Softly, nicely, Junie said, "Why don't you clean up this place. Clean yourself up. We'll take you back, you know that."

Cat raised his head. His eyes were red with anger. "I don't need you or Center Street. You'll be sorry. You'll all be sorry before I'm through with you. Maybe not today, or tomorrow, but you're going to hear from me, Junie Sando."

Junie left the yard, and the second he was out in the vacant lot, Cat slammed and bolted the gate and let out a deafening scream.

"I think we should wreck him up a little bit," Boris suggested. "Just so he can't get around too good. We don't need him gumming up the works."

"No," Junie said. "We'll put a tail on him. If he gets out of line, you 'heathens' can have him." Junie chuckled as the three of them started across the lot.

The warehouse, a large, rectangular, wood, two-story former pillow factory, was in Cherry Alley between Fifth and Sixth Streets. The Streeters had cleaned out the downstairs, painted it an off-white and kept it as a large meeting hall that could hold the entire organization. The extensive work was done on the second floor where carpenters divided it into three sections. The two outer portions were incorporated into special rooms and offices. Down at the far end was a medium-sized luxury apartment. The center section remained a wide, spacious hallway. Junie, Skippy and Boris came up the stairs and entered the main office to find Marty reading the Hudson Star.

"You're not going to like what I just read."

"What happened over at Lawyer Brink's?" Junie asked.

"He skipped town in the middle of the night. George Pugh met me over there, and we divided everything he left. We got the house, and Janet's going to have it fixed up and we'll rent it out. Now, about this article..."

"Later," said Junie. "Where's Frank Borzak?"

"He's around somewhere."

"Find him."

As Marty left the office, Junie took a deep sigh and plopped down in the chair behind the desk. "Tell me, Boris, how strong are your feelings toward Frank?"

"He belongs to my section, but he's not really Polish. His mother is Lithuanian or Latvian or some damn thing, and she's a dummy. He's not a real Pole. Polish people are proud and honest. Frank's just greedy and sneaky."

"What do you think should be done with him?"

"If I was you, I'd get rid of him. But you won't because he helped start this thing, and you don't stab your friends in the back. But I'm warning you, Junie, get rid of that creep, or he'll see you dead."

Teddy entered the office and asked, "What's up?"

"Frank Borzak."

"What did he do now?"

"You'll find out."

As Frank, Janet and Marty came into the office and closed the door, Frank sensed he was on the spot.

"How are things going, Frank?"

"Don't sugarcoat it, Junie."

"All right, I won't. I heard a rumor and I wanted to check with you on it. Did you take it upon yourself at the meeting yesterday to give the section leaders permission to kill?"

Frank gave Boris a dirty look and then glared around the room. "So that's it? The one person in this organization who really cares, and I'm called up. Maybe the rest of you don't give a shit if Nick starts hitting us one by one, but I do."

"Answer my question, Frank."

"You're hearing and taking everything out of context, Junie. Now, all I said was that *if* the Mob starts to strike back at us in any way, they will eliminate their assignments. I did not only what I thought was best, but what is the very best way to handle that situation should it arise. If I'm guilty of anything, anything at all, it may be just a little over-zealousness. But nothing more."

"Did you think, Frank," Junie said, "that if maybe one of the leaders was a little 'over-zealous' he might take it upon himself to hit one of them? Suppose they shoot at us to scare us and miss, should we strike back?"

"Of course not."

"Did you tell the leaders that?"

"They should know better."

"You should know better, Frank. You're the one who should have known better."

"I did what I know is best for Center Street."

"From now on you will not speak to any of the leaders on matters of policy. You will not hand out any orders or assignments to any members of the organization, and you will watch your step from here on in. Boris, since he's in your section, you will decide his punishment."

"Punishment?" Frank shouted. "What do you call what you just gave me?"

"I gave you a warning. Boris will decide your punishment."

"Now wait a minute. Boris is under me because I'm a member of the board."

"Not today, you're not," said Junie. "If you take your punishment well, we'll reconsider your status. But right now you have no power whatsoever."

"I don't mind telling you I don't like this at all," Frank said as fear of the punishment began to set in. "It isn't right because I didn't do anything, and he shouldn't have authority to punish me. I can take it, but I'm telling you I don't like it and I won't forget it."

"What's the punishment, Boris?" Junie asked.

"Seven lashes with a rubber hose."

"You son-of-a-bitch, Boris!" Frank spat.

"Seven lashes it is," said Junie, "but the sentence will be post-poned for the time-being and you'll be on probation. One miscue and Skippy McDonald and Bruce West will carry out the sentence. Now, go home and stay there until we send for you."

Frank was relieved, too relieved to speak, and simply bolted from the room. As everyone else began to leave the office, Marty took Junie aside. "I mentioned to you about the secret handshake not being clandestine enough, and I wanted to come up with a secret code word. I think I've got a cryptic formula and a great word."

"Good for you. But make it four words instead of just one."

Marty thought about it, burst into a wide grin and said, "Okay, okay, you're right. I will."

"I like your enthusiasm, Marty."

"Thank you, Junie. I really appreciate that. I mean it."

Nick Coletti had not touched his breakfast of sausage and eggs. He sat with his wife, Sally, and their daughter Rosanna while staring at the steps where his son Tony would come down to the dining room.

"Aren't you hungry, honey?" Sally asked.

Nick looked at her, forced a smile, tasted the scrambled eggs and immediately went back to looking for Tony.

"Rosanna has a dance class this morning," Sally announced proudly. Nick turned to the little girl, touched her hand and said, "What time, baby?"

The tiny, eight-year-old, bright-eyed brunette frowned in thought and guessed, "Ten-forty-five," and then looked up at her mother. "Is that right?"

"Perfect," said Sally.

Nick managed a smile, but continued to wait impatiently for Tony. "Why is he sleeping so late?"

"He's getting up," said Sally. "I just heard him."

"He shouldn't get into the habit of sleeping late during the summer, because he'll want to do it when school starts."

"We've never had a problem with Tony about getting up for school. He should enjoy his vacation. Besides, he has something to tell you."

"What?" Nick asked anxiously.

"Just let him tell you."

"You tell me," Nick said loudly. "I want to know what he's doing."

"All right," Sally said to calm him. "He's got a job."

"A job!? Doing what?"

"He's going to be working over at Mrs. Granowski's flower shop on Sixth Street."

"How did he get that job?"

"One of the other kids quit and told him about it," Sally explained. "I think it's wonderful that he wants to work. Shhh, here he comes."

Tony came bouncing down the stairs, skipped into the room, kissed his mother on the cheek, said, "Hi, Dad," and then took his seat. "What are you saying, Native Dancer?"

"Mommmm!" Rosanna cried. "I told him I didn't want him calling me that."

"Tony, now stop," Sally cautioned him.

"Tony?" Nick said.

"All right, all right."

"Tony, how did you get your job?"

Tony turned to his father, saw the cold, suspicious glare and stopped smiling. "What's wrong, Dad?"

"I asked you how you got that job."

"A kid told me about it."

"What kid?"

"A kid named Marty Politzsky."

"Where do you know this kid from?"

"From school," Tony said and stared back at his father.

"Don't I give you enough money?"

"Nick...?"

"You stay out of this!" Nick snapped at Sally. "Well, Tony, don't you get enough money from us?"

"Sure I do, but I'd rather have my own," Tony said, seemingly unafraid.

"I want to know about the kids in this town. I want to know who organized these kids. I want to know who-"

"Nick, what are you talking about?" Sally shouted while placing her arms protectively around Tony.

After a pause, Nick nodded toward Tony and said, "He knows. He knows damn well what I'm talking about. Don't you?"

"No, I don't, Dad. If I did, I'd tell you."

Nick leaned toward him and said softly, "You lying little bastard."

Sally snatched Tony up from the table while saying, "You kids go outside and play. Get out of here!"

When the children were out in the back yard, Sally stood seething, staring at Nick. "These are our children! What's the matter with you?"

Without looking up at Sally, Nick said, "He knows."

"What does he know!?" she yelled.

Calmly, Nick stood, walked over to Sally and softly, threateningly, he said, "That's what you'd better find out. I want you to find out what he knows, and you tell me. Because if you won't, I will."

Marty Politzsky opened the Hudson Star to the Mark Jansen editorial and began by saying, "He usually writes a sports column three times a week. His sister's husband owns the paper, otherwise who knows where he'd be."

"Probably back in Norristown, Pennsylvania," said Janet. "That's where he's from. He grew up there, graduated from high school and started to work for the local radio station WNAR as a sports announcer. They fired him after two years and then his sister, Nancy, suggested he come here to Hudson where she could put him to work. He's a fancy dresser, thinks he's hot stuff with the girls. But from what I hear, it's mostly talk."

"So what did he say in the column?" Junie asked Marty.

"At first he's talking about how great Hudson is," Marty began, "and then he says something about how nothing is sure, or safe, and there are many unnoticeable dangers that could destroy the tranquil peace of the Hudson Valley. And then he goes on 'It has been brought to this reporter's attention that the bloody and all too numerous amount of gang fights, or rumbles as the local hoodlums refer to them, are not taking place this summer. Everyone, needless to say, is extremely pleased with this. No one more than yours truly. But at what price peace, I ask. Have some of the teenagers of our fair city replaced the rumbles of the past summers with something far more injurious to our serene way of life? My inexhaustible research has revealed to me that there are four very bright, yet possibly dangerous teenagers in Hudson. For some mysterious reason, these four are not only socializing regardless of their different backgrounds, race, color, ethnic purity and social status, but seem to have formed a very close and closed social circle of their own. And, I ask, is there anything to the talk of all the teenagers of Hudson becoming part of one large para-military organization under the title of Center Street? Do you know where your child is right now? Who he, or she, is associating with and why? Do you know if your child is being guided, or misguided? These are the questions we as responsible citizens of Hudson, we as parents and we as Americans, must address ourselves to before it is too late. Mark Jansen.'"

"He's got to go," said Junie.

"No one is going to pay any attention to that drivel," Marty exclaimed.

"You're probably right, but I don't want him to have a soapbox. Call George Pugh and get him fired...today."

"Junie's right," said Janet.

"But his brother-in-law owns the paper."

"Tell George Pugh to find a way," Junie demanded, "or we will."

"Okay," Marty sighed. "I just hope we're not using ammunition we're going to need later."

Sally Coletti stood in the kitchen looking out into the back yard as Tony sat in the swing while watching Rosanna demonstrate her dancing. When Rosanna finished a pirouette, Tony applauded and yelled, "Bravo, bravo!"

"Tony," Sally called through the open window. "Will you come in here, please?"

"Keep practicing, kid," Tony said as he ran toward the house. Entering the kitchen he found his mother with an aggrieved look on her face.

"What's wrong, Mom?"

"Tony...?" she began and stopped.

"Dad and I don't like each other much, Mom."

Sally reached for Tony, and taking his face in her hands, she said, "Don't be bad, Tony, please!"

"I'm not being bad, Mom."

After a pause, Sally asked, "I know you don't get along, but does your father have anything to worry about?"

"What do you mean?"

"I want to know if your father has anything to worry about."

"In his line of work? Of course, he does."

"What are the teenagers going to do to him?"

Tony backed away from his mother and said, "I really don't know, Mom."

"Tony, are they going to harm your father?"

Shrugging and looking directly up at his mother, Tony said, "They don't want to. They just want peace and to find jobs for all us kids. That's all I know."

"Who organized the children?"

"All I know is what I told you, Mom. I really have to go now."

"Where?"

"To work. If I'm late I could get punished."

"Punished? Who will punish you?"

"Well, not really punished, but..."

"Who will punish you?"

"If I'm late I could get fired, Mom. It's my first day. Mrs. Granowski told me not to be late."

"I want to talk to Mrs. Granowski. What's her number?"

"I don't know."

"Sit down. I'll look it up in the phone book."

As Tony took a seat, Sally went to the kitchen wall phone and looked up the flower shop's number. She dialed, and when she asked Mrs. Granowski whether Tony was supposed to work there, the answer was yes and that he shouldn't be late.

Lowering the phone slowly, Sally turned to Tony and said, "Tell me what's going on."

"I'm not being bad, Mom. And I've told you all I know, honest."

Sally continued to stare at Tony for a moment and then went to him, hugged him and kissed his hair. "Don't be bad, Tony. Please don't be bad."

"I'm not, Mom, but I really got to go." He backed away then, turned and ran out of the house.

Nick Coletti had arrived at the Diamond Casino, taken Mario Carlucci's payment from the safe, sealed it an envelope and handed it to Nappy and Bummer to deliver it down to Brooklyn. Nappy and Bummer no sooner got into their 1958 Chrysler, started it and released the emergency brake, when the four wheels moved and fell off the car. A moment later an explosion sent the hood flying thirty feet into the air. The two men sat stunned, waiting to die. When nothing else happened, Nappy and Bummer rushed out of the car. Nick and Lido, standing at the back door of the casino, witnessed what had happened. Looking around, Nick spied three boys, Donald Morrant, Bobby West and Jeff Gershon watching through binoculars on a rooftop a half a block away. Satisfied with their work and Nick's reaction, the three teenagers lowered their glasses and disappeared.

"What do we do now, boss?" Nappy asked.

After a pause, Nick said softly, "We meet with them tomorrow morning."

The Borzak family, father, mother and seven children, including Frank, the middle child, lived in a sturdy, two-story house in the far end of the Robinson Street section of Hudson. Mother Borzak kept an immaculately clean house and was seen at least once a week on her hands and knees scrubbing down the porch and front steps. Frank's father, a diligent, railroad worker, had built a reinforced plank fence at the rear of the backyard because of a steep forty-foot drop leading down to the softball diamonds and the clay banks beyond. There were many long-winded, scary tales about the dark, mysterious clay banks. Some spoke of bodies being buried there. And some of the tales were true.

Frank Borzak came directly home after his trial at Center Street. He was lying on his bed and staring out at the clay banks. When his mother, Mrs. Sophie Borzak, entered the room, she could feel the pain her son was suffering. The deaf mute woman asked in sign language if he was all right. Frank nodded that he was. His mother wanted to touch him, maybe even caress him, but Frank was never a warm, responsive child, even though at that moment he might have welcomed it. But not knowing this, Mrs. Borzak smiled, nodded goodbye and left the room. Frank continued to stare out of the window while trying to think of anything to relieve the pain of his fall from grace with Center Street. Some relief came to him by firmly believing that this wasn't the end. As long as Center Street existed he would continue to plot and plan and believe that some day he would have all of that power in his hands.

Helene Mulzer, the large, blonde, teenage girl, lived with her family next door to the Mayor of Hudson. He was a Conservative Republican by the name of Cameron Brown. Helene, Janet Hammond and Cindy Wells were in the basement of the Mulzer home, listening and secretly recording a telephone conversation between Mayor

Brown and Nick Coletti. The Mayor was complaining about the small amount of graft he was receiving under the circumstances.

Nick said he was having some serious problems of his own, but would see what he could do. When the Mayor hung up, Cindy Wells smiled and winked at Helene. Janet told Cindy to make a copy of the tape and to get it over to George Pugh.

12

Teddy: "Now that I think back, most of the adults, not all, but
most were purposely, intentionally unaware of what was
going on with us. It reminds me of the German citizens
who claimed to be unaware of what was happening in
their country back in the thirties and forties. The people
of Hudson were a hard-working, simple class of people
who merely didn't wish to make waves, especially when
it came to their own children."

The local newspaper, the Hudson Star, occupied the entire large,
two-story, brick building on the northeastern corner of Fourth and
Main Streets. Horace Woodward was the founder, owner and edi-
tor of the small (twenty-five workers) monopoly. The Star was the
only printed news source in Columbus County. Horace, now in his
late sixties, was an obese man, scruffy, bored, yet fiercely independent. He was a proud individual, a moderate with a liberal attitude
toward his political opponents. Somewhere along the way he had
picked up a progressively heavy drinking problem. More and more,
his wife, Nancy Jansen Woodward, who was thirty years his junior,
was taking over the business. It was shy, dour, plain Nancy who
had taken the telephone call from George Pugh and was instantly
concerned when the counselor said it was imperative he speak with
Horace. "Well, if it's really important," Nancy said, "I guess it's best
you come right on over."

The first person George saw when he entered the lobby of the news building was dapper, red-haired Mark Jansen who was all smiles because of the notoriety he was receiving from his editorial. "Hey, Georgie baby, did you read my column?"

"Yes, as a matter of fact, I did."

Putting his arm around George's shoulders, Mark spoke privately while saying, "Do me a favor, will you? While you're in there, see what you can do for me. I'm not getting what I deserve. If Horace wants to keep me, he should protect his interest. Right? You do this for me and I'll owe you one, Georgie baby."

George nodded and walked upstairs to Horace Woodward's office.

"Well, George, what's so damned important?"

"May I sit?"

"Suit yourself," said Horace.

George took a seat, looked around the drab, cluttered office and noticed that absolutely nothing had changed in twenty years. "How's your gin holding out?"

"Just fine, George. Just fine."

"Let's face it, Horace, I know you and I have not been the closest of friends over the years, but Lord knows we haven't been enemies either."

"We haven't been enemies," Horace repeated.

"Now, when someone came to me and said that Horace Woodward was in dire need of financial assistance, my greedy gut started to churn and my mouth got wet thinking of the ways I could rip this place right out of your hands. But then I stopped and said, 'George Pugh, what in the hell is wrong with you? What has Horace Woodward ever done to you?' Well, I'm here to apologize for such thoughts and to offer my services free of charge. I know, I was informed by a rat that you have several mortgages on your home and this place is in debt right up to your neck. Now, all I'm asking, Horace, from the bottom of my heart, is that if you decide you need help, you will come to me first. What I know, what I have been told will stay with me. What this other person does is his business, but my lips are sealed."

Horace was stunned and tried not to show it. "Who told you all that?"

"That is not the purpose of my visit, Horace. These little pipsqueaks who run around stabbing their friends and relatives in the back need to be run out of town. I'm here as a friend. This town needs you, Horace. This newspaper is the cornerstone of the entire culture of Hudson and this area of the Hudson Valley. And you have my word that if I can help you in any way, you will remain at the head of this newspaper until you and you alone say different."

"That's very kind of you, George...if you mean it."

"I'll put it in writing if it will ease your mind."

"I never thought of you as being..."

"I know what you mean, Horace. I know what people think about me in this town. But I am not one of these people who goes around saying things to hurt their sisters and brothers and people who are more than kind to them. I want to tell you so badly, but my conscience won't allow it. But believe me, you'll find it out. I know you'll know what to do with that little mealy-mouthed back stabber. Imagine him coming to me and saying he knows of a way to take over the Star from Horace Woodward. Hell, this paper wouldn't even look the same without you, much less read the same. If I was a younger man I would have pulled his arms out of their sockets."

"I appreciate this, George."

"Then will you promise to come to me first if you need help?"

"I swear I will."

George stood up and shook hands with Horace. "Give it a day or two and you'll know your Judas. Clean house, Horace. Cut back. I'm not known as being a very religious man myself, but I recall from my Bible School days that in Matthew 10:36 it says: 'And a man's foe shall be those of his own household.' In other words, sometimes those who pretend to be closest to us are crapping on the front porch and calling it mud."

13

Teddy: "It happened on the morning we were preparing to meet Nick Coletti. Junie took me aside and said, 'We must remain nonviolent, Teddy. We must settle our differences through diplomacy. Being prepared for war must only act as a deterrent to war. We must never, ever unleash the power of Center Street on anyone.' When I asked, 'What if push comes to shove?' he replied, 'Only a stupid, mad dog would ever push us that far.'"

Tuesday morning, July 3, 1959, turned into a scorcher. As if the night before wasn't enough (it was seventy-four degree at 2:00 a.m.), the temperature was already at ninety-two by eight o'clock.

The Streeters who were to take part in the morning meeting got very little sleep, and Nick Coletti didn't fare much better. The Warriors to be involved were told to meet with Junie at the headquarters by 9:00 a.m. and to be on time. They were. Teddy and a labor crew had worked late into the night preparing the office for the meeting. The room led to the fire escape. The soldiers would cover every step of the way from both ends of the alley to and including the inside of the headquarters. The office where the meeting was to take place was halved by a wall of barbed wire with only a small window-like opening for Nick Coletti's face. The six teenagers,

Marty, Janet, Teddy, Frank, Butch and Augie, would be safely behind the wire sitting or standing around the desk. There was a heavy, meditative silence prevailing among the teenagers as they waited.

"You know something?" Butch said. "We ought to make a deal. Something that says if they get any of us, the rest of us will get them."

"A revenge vow," Marty explained.

"And we should write it in blood," Frank suggested.

"Yeah!" said Augie.

"I really don't think it's necessary to drain our veins," Janet stated. "A single drop of blood from each of our index fingers will suffice."

Janet took a piece of paper and pen from the desk drawer and started to write. She entitled it: "The Center Street Pact."

As Janet wrote, she spoke, "We, the undersigned, do solemnly swear in the presence of Almighty God and our dearest friends, that if any of the undersigned are murdered, the remaining members of the group, on pain of severe punishment, must-"

"No," Frank interrupted. "On pain of death."

Janet looked at the others. When no one objected, she said, "Okay. On pain of death, will respond likewise and take vengeance on the antagonist. This we do so solemnly swear."

"I'll sign first," said Butch.

After the other four had signed, they all turned to Teddy West who remained, as usual, against the wall with his arms folded.

"Your turn, Teddy," said Augie.

Teddy shrugged and said, "Why not?"

After Teddy had completed the list, Augie asked, "What about the blood?"

"Does anyone have a pin?" Marty asked.

"I have a safety pin," Augie said and removed the pin that had replaced the button on his shirt cuff. Frank took out a pack of matches, burned the end of the pin, wiped it clean and said, "Who's first?"

"I'll go first," Butch said and closed his eyes, grimaced and extended his index finger.

Frank jabbed him quickly. Butch yelled, "Ouch" and then looked down as his finger began to spot blood. Placing the finger next to his name, he said, "I do solemnly swear in the sight of Almighty God."

Each one followed in quick succession. When the ritual was complete, Janet folded the paper, placed it in an envelope, sealed it and locked it in the desk drawer.

Nick and his men were waiting in the old Diamond Casino office when the telephone rang at precisely ten o'clock.

"Good morning, Saint Nicholas."

"Where do we go?" Nick asked.

"That's not a very warm greeting."

"I'm not in a very warm mood."

"You never are. There's a warehouse in Cherry Alley between Fifth and Sixth Streets. Come up to the second floor, third office on the right."

Nick hung up. "Let's go."

The limousine was watched from the moment it left Diamond Street until it came up the alley and stopped in front of the warehouse. As the men entered, Lido was casing the place inch by inch. When they reached the top of the stairs they were met by a group of soldiers standing in a long, straight line on the left from one end of the hall to the other. The boys were silent as Nick, Lido, Bummer and Nappy moved down to the third office on the right. They entered, walked up to the barbed wire and heard the door being locked behind them. Nick gazed around the room, chuckled and then looked directly and penetratingly at each teenager. "Don't tell me this is a shakedown."

"No. Merely a business arrangement," Marty announced.

Nick chuckled. "A business arrangement? I don't conduct business with punks."

"Do you like what's been happening to you?"

"No, I don't like it, and it's going to stop or a couple of you are going to come up missing."

"Now why does that sound distinctly like a threat?"

"Because it is," said Nick. "I've taken all I'm going to off you brats!"

"You can't touch us, and you know it," Marty continued.

"That may be true, but you all have parents. Your mothers and fathers are going to start paying the price for your games."

Janet leaned forward and said, "So could Sally, Rosanna and Tony."

Nick snickered and said, "Mark Jansen says you're all smart. If you are, you better be smart enough to know I ain't taking any more crap."

"Do you want to talk business or not?" Marty asked.

"There's nothing to talk about."

"We don't want things to continue the way they are, Nick, because we've got more important things to do than playing childish games with you. So if you'll agree to pay us a certain amount every week, we'll stop."

"The answer is a flat no!"

"But why, Nick? You can afford it, and you can't afford to have us against you."

"You're going to stop," Nick said, "or you're going to wish to God you had."

"Okay, we'll play it your way."

"All right, open the door and let us out."

"Oh, yes, I almost forgot. Lido, do you recognize this?" Marty asked and pulled a white towel off a .32 automatic Beretta that was on the desk.

"Hey, that's my rod. I lost it a couple of days ago."

"You didn't lose anything, stupid. We took it while you slept, and it has your fingerprints all over it."

"So what?" said Nick.

"So...the one thing you can't do and get away with is kill a child. You can kill each other and no one cares. Once in a while you can get away with killing some adults, regular citizens. But if one kid is killed with that gun, you're through. Washed up, and not only here, but everywhere."

"Suppose we take that gun right now?" Lido snarled.

"God, you're stupid! You try that and those soldiers are going to come in here and beat you to death."

There was a long pause and then Nick said, "So what are you saying?"

"That's better," said Marty. "We know almost to the penny the amount of money you're making off the rackets. We also assume you were smart enough to bring the thousand with you that we mentioned. We'll take that, and every Monday morning you'll deliver the same amount in an envelope into the mail slot in the downstairs door."

"A thousand a week!" Nick exclaimed. "I can't afford that."

"You can't afford not to."

"This is ridiculous. I don't even know why I'm standing here listening to this."

"You're standing here because you don't have a choice."

"They're bluffing, Nick," Lido said.

"Of course, they're bluffing! If you punks kill a kid, you're the murderers, not us."

"With that gun?" Marty asked. "You don't really think they'll take your word over ours, do you?"

Nick glared at Marty. "Suppose you're the kid who gets killed?"

This riled the other Streeters, and they moved uneasily. Marty remained calm, lowered his head, and when he looked up, he said softly, "Kill me, I'd gladly die for my friends."

"No," Frank shouted. "Kill me. I'd gladly die for my friends."

Butch chuckled, "No, kill me. I'd gladly die for my friends."

The curtain in the back of the room slid open and a small, seven-year-old blonde girl with bright blue eyes and a round, cherubic face, who was wearing polio braces, began to hobble forward as she said, "No. Kill me. I'd gladly die for my friends."

Her name was Debbie Ryan and as she labored forward, the four men looked down at her in shock and disbelief. She stopped at a certain point in the room. Frank lifted the white towel and hung it on the wall next to her head.

"Now, we're about to see how heartless you guys really are," said Marty. "Because I'm going to pick up that gun, Janet is going to count to ten, and I'm going to blow this little girl's blood and brains all against that towel so we can give it to the F.B.I."

"Just wait until your big time friends in New York and Chicago hear about this," Butch laughed.

"Don't be ignorant, Nick," said Frank. "What have you got to lose? A thousand a week doesn't even make a dent into what you guys are making."

"He's a jerk," Janet added. "You put a chimpanzee in a five-hun-dred-dollar suit, you've still got an ape."

"All right," said Augie, "let's get it over with."

Marty lifted the gun in a handkerchief, walked over to Debbie and placed the barrel at her temple. "Start counting, Janet."

"One..."

"Hold it, Marty," Teddy spoke for the first time. "They know you're not going to do it."

"But I will," Marty tried to sound convincing.

"No you won't and they know it."

Nick and the others started laughing. "Okay, kids, let us out of here."

"Frank...you do it."

Everyone looked at Teddy.

"Teddy, I, ah..." Marty tried to speak.

"Go ahead, Frank," Teddy continued. "You do it."

Nick Coletti looked at Frank and he didn't like the malicious smile the boy had as he took the Beretta from Marty. Frank continued to smile as he looked at the men and then stopped smiling, turned and pointed the gun at Debbie.

"And, Frank," Teddy called over to him, "I want you to do it. I want you to kill her."

As Frank pushed the point of the barrel against Debbie's head, she began to cry.

"Start counting, Janet," Teddy said.

"Okay," Janet sighed. "One...two..."

Frank cocked the hammer on the automatic and pushed it even firmer against Debbie's temple.

"Three...four..."

"Give them the money," Nick said almost inaudibly.

"Don't be a sucker, Nick!" Lido shouted. "He's not going to shoot her!"

Nick screamed, "Give them the goddamn money!"

Reluctantly, slowly, Lido reached into his inside jacket pocket, pulled out the envelope and tossed it through the barbed wire and onto the desk. Janet opened the envelope, counted it and said, "Okay. But don't forget...every Monday in the slot in the door."

"Okay, okay," Nick said trying not to show his relief. "But this is it. Don't try to take it any further. And I want it to stay with just you kids. Don't bring any grown-ups in on it, or there's going to be trouble."

"Don't threaten us," Janet warned him.

Nick threw up his hands. "No threats. No threats, lady, just a business arrangement. Right?"

When they didn't answer, Nick snickered and looked at each of the kids. Then he chuckled, shrugged and turned to leave.

After the men were gone, Junie Sando came rushing into the room. "You guys okay?"

"We're a thousand dollars a week okay," said Marty.

They all acted as if they didn't notice Debbie making her way laboriously back toward the curtain as they congratulated each other. And then suddenly they all ran over, lifted her into the air, hugged, tickled and cheered her as she laughed.

14

Teddy: "A lot of people have asked me about that meeting. Whether or not I would have allowed Frank to shoot if Janet had reached the count of ten. I simply assumed it wouldn't come to that. Sherm, I don't mean to give you the impression that all of the members were as militant and capable and efficient as we were, because they weren't. Most were teenagers and they did what kids will do, show up late, fall asleep on their jobs, and some didn't even show up at all. I'll tell you, if this thing had gone on for more than a few weeks, I think most of them would have become bored, said forget it and gone back home to their parents."

"I'm cutting back," Horace Woodward said as he stared out at the golden cross on the Fourth Street Methodist Church.

"But why me?" Mark Jansen whined. "Have you forgot that I'm your brother-in-law?"

"Now how could I forget something like that? But as you are all too well aware, I'm mortgaged right up to my gin drinking ass with no relief in sight. There are certain things around here that are expendable and, unfortunately for you, you're one of them."

Mark, who had been standing in the center of the room, rushed to take a chair. "I don't believe this. I do something magnificent for the paper and I get fired."

"First of all, your editorial was not all that earth-shattering, and–"

"Bullshit, Horace!" Mark shouted. "That's all everybody in this town is talking about."

"...and second of all, that is not why you're being laid off."

"Don't hand me that laid-off crap! You're firing me for good and you know it!"

"Have it your way," Horace said without looking at him.

"I want to know, Horace," Mark continued to shout. "I want to know the truth of why you're getting rid of me!"

Horace sipped his gin as Nancy rushed into the office. "What's going on in here? We can hear you two all over the building."

"Horace just fired me," Mark whimpered.

"Fired you? What in the name of God for?"

"Ask him!"

"Horace, why in the name of God did you fire Mark?"

"First of all, I didn't fire him in the name of God. I fired him in the name of expediency. I have to cut back somewhere and he's expendable."

Nancy chuckled and said, "Oh, Horace darling, if we need to cut back, there are many other areas we can do it without firing Mark."

"Well, maybe there are, and I'll be sure to check thoroughly into them. But for right now he goes and he knows damn well why."

Nancy turned to Mark, who said, "What the hell are you talking about, Horace?"

"Figure it out, Mark. Take the rest of the day and figure it out,"

Mark grimaced as he said, "It's the kids. It's those goddamn kids, isn't it, Horace?"

"Kids? What damn kids?"

"Those teenagers down at Center Street."

"Nancy, I do believe your brother has gone utterly mad."

"They did it!" Mark yelled. "They did it, those little bastards did it. Horace, I'm telling you they have got to be stopped."

Nancy and Horace were both staring at Mark in astonishment.

"Mark, what in the name of God are you talking about?"

"I do believe you're taking your editorial a tad too seriously, son," Horace said and chuckled.

Balling his hands into fists, Mark tried to get control of himself.

"Horace, you've got to tell me how they got you to do it. Please, Horace!"

After staring at Mark for a long moment, Horace threw his head back, laughing as he said, "You've gone completely off your rocker. If you think, if you honestly believe that the teenagers had you fired, then why don't you just go on over and ask them. And then come back, no, no, call me and let me know how they did it. Now, if you can prove they did it, I'll rehire you with a one-hundred-percent raise in pay and give you a daily column."

"You're making fun of me, Horace. But I'm going to stop those kids if I have to go all the way to Albany or Washington."

Nancy remained in the office after Mark had gone. As Horace turned back to the window, she said, "What is it, Horace?"

"Your brother's got a big mouth, Nancy. He went blabbing to George Pugh everything about my finances. I don't need anyone..." He stopped and turned to Nancy and then continued, "I don't need anyone who isn't loyal to me." Horace then sipped his gin and turned back to the cross.

Janet Hammond and Marty Politzsky were in the warehouse office when the door burst open and Mark rushed in. "I was told by some girl downstairs that whoever was up here is in charge."

Janet and Marty said nothing.

"I can't believe you two are mixed up in this thing. I know what you're doing. I know what your plans are, and I know damn well that you had me fired. Why are you doing this, Janet? Don't you have any idea what can happen? How much danger you're in?"

When Janet and Marty remained silent, Mark pleaded with them to stop it now. "You're both more than intelligent enough to know what can happen. God, why can't you see what you're doing?"

Shaking his head, Mark cursed under his breath and left the room.

"George Pugh is really on the ball, isn't he," said Janet.

When Junie and Teddy entered the office, Janet told them that Mark Jansen was just there.

"I know. We put Jeff Gershon on his tail."

"We have some other problems as well," Janet said.

"What is it?" Junie asked.

"At the rate we're going money-wise, with you planning on giving the kids a raise, we're going to be dead broke in less than a month."

"What happened to all the money that was in the Center Street account?"

"Junie, we've got money now, but with you giving them a raise, it's doubling our payroll."

"The raise is important, Janet."

"I know," she said, and then scratching an eyebrow she added, "there is one solution to all our financial problems."

"What's that?"

"After we run Nick out of town, we could keep the casinos and the houses going for just a week or two; and we'll come out way ahead."

Junie was silent. After a moment he turned to Teddy and asked, "What do you think?"

"It wouldn't hurt, I guess, as long as it's only for a week or two."

"That's all we would need," Janet assured them. "We could get that gambler, Jack Losse, to help us."

Junie was deep in thought. "I don't like it."

"If we want to keep the organization together and give the workers a raise, we don't have a choice."

"We can do it," Teddy said. "Just fourteen days and then we shut them down for good."

"All right," Junie finally agreed. "We'll try it."

Having struck out a few times, Mark Jansen pulled his Buick up in front of Principal Rockford's house on Fairlane Avenue and ran up to the front door. After ringing the bell four times, he pounded on the door. Nel Rockford, a huge, stocky woman who was infamous for ruling Hudson High School like a maximum security prison, heard the pounding and came around to see who it was. "What in the world is wrong with you, Mark?"

"I'm sorry, Miss Rockford, but something has come up and I have to talk to you."

Nel, who was dressed in a pair of overalls, stripped off her work gloves as she made her way up to the porch. "You don't have to bang my door in, do you?"

"I'm sorry, but once you hear what I have to say, you'll see how urgent it is."

"All right," Nel said and opened the door. "You may as well come on in."

Nel took a seat at the dining room table. "Well, let's hear it."

Mark sat and began, "Did you happen to read my column?"

"No, I was out of town for a few days, but someone told me about it."

"Never mind. What I was warning everyone about is beginning to happen."

Nel smiled while saying, "The teenagers stopped the gang wars, put everyone to work, and you think they're going to take over the country?"

"Well, not exactly, but definitely Hudson."

"But that's preposterous, Mark."

"It won't sound so preposterous once you hear this line-up. Marty Politzsky."

"That is absolutely ridiculous. Marty is one of the most intelligent, well-mannered young men in this town."

"I know he is, and that's why this is so serious. The other two boys are Frank Borzak and Teddy West."

"Now that I can believe, though I doubt Marty would be caught dead in their company."

"Well, he is, and constantly. And if that isn't enough for you, the fourth member is Janet Hammond."

"Janet Hammond!? Mark, this is absolutely ludicrous. Janet has been working in my office for the last two years."

"I'm telling you the truth, Miss Rockford. These four have formed the rest of the teenagers in Hudson into an army, and who knows what they have planned."

"Have you talked to Police Chief Madden about this?"

"I went to see him, but his secretary swore he wasn't in. I'm almost sure he was."

"What about the mayor?"

"He wouldn't listen to me."

"Why?"

"If you really want to know, I think they already have him."

"But how?"

Mark frowned and said he didn't know.

After a contemplative and angry thought, Nel said, "Even though that Frank Borzak is a smart little bastard, I've never liked him. And Teddy West thinks he's so goddamn slick. I'll have both of them in the Coxsackie Reform School if they mess around with me or my two prize students."

Mayor Cam Brown was in his office, a rather imposing and elegant room for a small-town politician, with hardwood floors and a rosewood desk. He was a tall, dark-haired man, insecure to the point of being paranoid. Though he was the last of the city officials to accept graft from Nick Coletti, once he began, he was constantly on the take and always in need of more. Turning in his green leather, swivel chair, he looked proudly out over the city of Hudson and began to compose his Fourth of July speech when the phone call came from Nel Rockford.

"Well, hey, Nel. I thought you were gone for the summer."

"I wouldn't miss your Fourth of July oration for anything in the world, Mayor."

"It's going to be a good one this year. Unemployment is at an all-time low, construction is up, crime is down, the fiscal-"

"Cam, what I am calling about is the column Mark Jansen wrote the other day."

Mayor Brown was struck silent. Choosing his words carefully, he said, "I see. So Mark is over there bothering you with that, is he?"

"If what Mark says is true, there are two-"

"I told Mark to go see Chief Madden. Now why didn't he?"

"He said he couldn't get in touch with Tom. And he also said that he thinks they have somehow got to you."

"Of course, they have," said Cam. "I'm sitting here right now chained to my chair while they torture me and rob my office. Nel, call Tom. He's handling this whole thing. Believe me, it is nowhere near what Mark is concerned about. I've checked into it thoroughly and the children have merely found jobs for most of the kids and have put a permanent stop to those horrible gang wars we've had every summer. Now what's wrong with that?"

"Mark's afraid there's a lot more to it."

"Then that is strictly a police matter. See you tomorrow, Nel." Mayor Brown hung up, hesitated a moment, lifted the phone to dial someone, changed his mind, cursed under his breath and slammed the receiver onto the cradle.

"Well, Miss Rockford, do you see what I mean?" Mark Jansen was saying as Nel was deep in thought.

"I can't believe it."

"I'm glad to see someone is starting to take notice."

"Well, dammit," Nel snapped, "if Chief Madden won't talk to you, he's sure as hell going to talk to me, or I'm going to know why!"

The dozen or so brothels, quaint, one-family, wood or shingled buildings, were interspersed with regular homes on both sides of Diamond Street between Third, Fourth and Fifth Streets. Hudson's most lucrative industry hit its peak in the late 1950s. Many of the older, experienced women lost part of their incomes because once some of the college girls around the state and down in New York City heard about the "amazingly easy" money to be made, there was a parade of them sneaking into town to work weekends. All were pretty, momentarily innocent and gullible young soubrettes brought into the business by a friend who had tried it. They were quickly taken under the protective wing of the madame: usually old, calloused matriarchs who guarded, nurtured and jealously protected their "Cherries," these tireless, desirable, fresh, clean, puerile gold mines who often worked nonstop for two days and nights and would turn over as much as sixty percent of their earnings. Butch Charles once said of the part-time prostitutes, "Them young chicks sell more trim than the law allows!"

The girls would be driven into town early Friday evenings and delivered to the houses through back alleys. The decor of every brothel was gaudy, brightly colored and quite often tasseled and muddled in designs of heirlooms, antiques and Montgomery Ward specials. The air was invariably heavy, sweetish, filled with a variety of perfumes probably no more expensive than rose water. The odor was neither pleasant nor necessarily offensive, but it was pervading and exclusively peculiar to the houses. Perhaps due to the environment and the ambience, it was a particular smell that one could never forget.

Attorney George Pugh was riding high during this time because of the despotic powers granted him by Center Street. In the waiting room he was sitting on a large, plush, pink sofa with Gertrude Allison, the number one Madame of Hudson. Gert was a well-rounded, red-haired, tough-looking woman with a pockmarked face that she tried in vain to cover with powder and make-up and detract from with large, black protruding eyelashes and bright red lipstick. Sitting in the dimly-lit parlor across from George and Gert was a shy, elderly gentleman in a bulky wool suit and tie. He was speaking in private with an anxious young strumpet. It was obviously his first visit to a whorehouse because he was embarrassed and pitiably nervous while trying to keep the girl from pawing him. He kept looking around the room to see if anyone was watching. When he looked up this time it was because two leggy harlots, wearing nothing but thigh-length, silk night jackets and high heel shoes, came laughing and talking through the room. The young strumpet had to place her hand on his face and spin his head back around to get his attention.

Taking a deep drag on a Chesterfield, Gert Allison exhaled noisily and said, "I'll be glad when Nick is gone, but I still think them kids got something to do with this."

"Come on, Gert," George pleaded, "would I be doing all this work for a bunch of snot-nosed brats?"

"Then why can't you tell me who's really backing you?"

"Because the gentleman prefers to remain anonymous. All we want to know is, will you go along with us?"

"And you say I'll only pay you half of what we've been giving Nick?"

"That's right," said George. "So will you go along with us?"

"I told you I would. I just don't want no funny business, and I don't want to deal with no kids."

George chuckled as the phone on the coffee table rang and Gert answered it. "Hello."

"Miss Allison, this is Nel Rockford, the principal of Hudson High School. I must speak with Police Chief Tom Madden. Now, I know he's there, so don't deny it. Just put him on the phone."

"I have no intention of denying it, Miss Rockford, but Chief Madden might. Hold on."

"I'll handle it," George said. "Where is he?"

"In the first room down the hall with Kitty."

George walked down to the room and heard the sounds of love-making. The bed springs were squeaking, the brass head railing was banging against the wall, Big Tom Madden could be heard grunting and groaning, and Kitty, who was a professional to say the least, was responding in kind with the usual and well-practiced "Ooohs" and "Aw-babies."

George, waiting until their amore was at its fever pitch and about to explode, pounded on the door and entered without waiting to be invited. Tom Madden jumped off the raven-haired, blue-eyed Kitty while snatching the covers up to his chin. "What the hell is wrong with you, George!?"

"Sorry to interrupt, Tom, Miss Kitty, but it seems you have an urgent phone call out in the parlor, Chief."

"Phone call? Who would call me here?"

"Nel Rockford," George said simply while gazing fondly at Kitty who remained exposed down to her thighs.

"Nel Rockford? You interrupted me for Nel Rockford? Are you insane?"

"I wouldn't have bothered you, Tom, but she said it was urgent."

"Urgent, my ass!" Tom said as he got out of bed, pulled on his pants and left the room.

George smiled at Kitty, moved toward her and shook his head in amazement. And then slowly, gingerly he ran his hand over her cheek, shoulder and breast that was still heaving from the lovemaking. George then took the pink nipple between his thumb and forefinger, softly massaging it.

"Why don't you ever come here and see me sometime, George?"

"Whenever I come here, it's to see you, Kitty."

"But you never take me to a room so I can make you feel good. Why?"

"Because if I ever did, I'd never go home to my wife."

Chief Madden was on the parlor phone listening to Nel Rockford.

"Now you know, Tom, if any of this is true, we should look into it."

"I've already looked into it, Nel, and there's nothing to it."

"But, Tom, if Janet Hammond and Martin-"

"Nel!" Tom shouted. "Did Mark tell you he is no longer with the Star? That his own brother-in-law, Horace Woodward, fired him?"

When Nel didn't answer, Tom said, "I can tell that he didn't. It's because of wild accusations like this that he lost his job. My suggestion would be to let me and the police department handle this. I have every intention of talking to every one of those parents before the week is out. Now, if you want to sit around and help Mark Jansen feel sorry for himself, that's your business. Just don't be bothering me or the other city officials with his garbage." Tom waited for a reply. When Nel remained silent, he said, "Have a good Fourth, Nel. I'll see you in front of City Hall tomorrow morning."

George Pugh had moved over to the bedroom door as Tom came charging back into the room, removed his pants and hurried into bed. "Well?" George asked.

"I took care of it," Tom replied and waved for George to leave the room.

"You still want me to do that thing for you tonight?" Kitty called to George. George smiled and nodded as he departed.

Nel Rockford had been sitting silently in thought for a full minute after speaking with Police Chief Madden. Mark Jansen waited impatiently for her to say something. Finally he asked, "What did he say?"

Nel awoke and said, "He feels we should let him and the police department handle it. He also said he'll talk to the parents."

Mark laughed wryly while shaking his head. "Can't you see we're being brushed off? Somebody has to care about what is happening."

Nel looked over at Mark and asked, "When is your next editorial coming out?"

"I'm no longer with the paper. Those dear, sweet and wonderful teenagers had me fired. I know it sounds ridiculous, but it's the truth. Please, please believe me, Nel."

"I didn't say I didn't believe you."

"You didn't say you did either," Mark said, knowing he had lost her.

"Look, Mark, they'll all be back at my school in two months, and then I'll check into it thoroughly."

"Two months? Don't you realize what they could do in two months? Look what they've done in no time at all."

"Why don't you let Chief Madden handle it, Mark?"

"No. No, I won't," he said. "I'm going to Albany. I'm going to tell the F.B.I. And if they won't listen, I'll go to Washington if I have to."

"You sound so silly, Mark."

"I know," he conceded. "And all of you are going to look so damn silly when the truth is finally known. I just hope someone will listen to me before it goes too far. Goodbye, Miss Rockford."

15

Teddy: "You're right, Joseph, we did have the town in a tizzy. Some of the teenagers were questioned by their parents, but how could the adults complain? Most of them had never seen their offspring so happy, contented and involved. The kids knew exactly what to say. Janet had briefed them thoroughly. Their job was to convince their parents of the good we had done. The kid would go on to say how he had improved as an individual and how all of it would help tremendously in school come September. And if they needed further proof, Junie would pay a personal visit to the parents where he never failed to completely charm the mother and relieve the father of any anxieties. We decided to give a party. As I look back, the party could very well have been the turning point that summer. Celebrations can be terribly misleading."

Pink was the color of the day. Every boy had a pink shirt and every girl a pink dress, skirt or blouse. The party was to begin at eight o'clock, but the hall was filling up by seven-thirty. Jack Losse, the poker player from Flatbush, didn't know what to expect when George Pugh came into O'Brien's Pool Hall to say he had a deal for him, and invited the card shark to a party at a place called Center

Street. Jack was suspicious, especially when they turned into Cherry Alley. But this alley was different, not dark, nor dreary, but clean, paved and extremely well-lit. "What the hell?" is the only thing Jack could say. He was a tall, well-built, handsome man with dark features. They entered the warehouse and went upstairs as the sound of the party began. When George opened the door to the richly furnished apartment, Jack stepped inside and said, "Hey, this is nice." Junie Sando and Tuck Ryan were waiting. After introducing Jack Losse, George fixed and served some drinks. Looking into his glass of Wild Turkey, Jack remarked, "I never bet the farm, George, so tell me where I fit in?"

"You know gambling. You can stop playing in those penny-ante games and start yourself a large savings account."

Jack chuckled. "I see. You gentlemen are going to take over Nick's operations, and you want me to help you with the casinos."

"No. We want you to run the casinos any way you see fit. As long as you make a profit, of course."

"Of course," Jack said. "There is one little thing I wonder if you've taken into consideration."

"Nick has no idea there are any adults in on this thing. The teen-agers have met with him, and he's now paying them a thousand dollars each and every week. They've got him right where they want him."

"Today they do, but even an orange can only be squeezed so much before the juice runs dry."

"You only live once, Jack. Why do you insist on dying of a heart attack in a two dollar five-card-stud game, when we're offering you a chance to catch a star?"

"There is one other thing I'd better explain to you," said Junie. "It's not going to be a long range thing. We're going to take over, run the operations for a short while just to put some cash in all our pockets, and then we're going to clean it up."

"That's very honorable," Jack said and looked over at George Pugh. "Are those your plans, too?"

"Junie's the boss here. So what do you say, Jack?"

Jack sipped his drink, looked at the men and replied, "The lodgings are splendid, the drink is the very best, the meals are sufficient, but man cannot live by bread alone."

George smiled as he, Junie and Tuck stood up and silently left the room. Jack sat perplexed and wary. He didn't know what to expect. After the longest minute he had ever endured, the door to the bedroom opened suddenly and Jack jumped up, dropping his glass to the floor. Kitty, wearing only a transparent, black negligee, stood in the doorway and said, "Welcome, Jack."

The Center Street party was now in full swing. The capable band was rocking out with "Night Train" and most of the kids were dancing. Sitting at a table against a far wall were Teddy West, Frank Borzak, who was there at Junie's orders, and Janet Hammond with her quiet, egghead boyfriend who wore black specs and a very formal dark suit, pink shirt and bow tie. Noticing how dour Frank was looking, Teddy said, "What have you got a bug up your ass about? You should be happy. Isn't this what you comrades want, a happy workers' state? Everyone working and living happily under one Politburo?"

"You believe that, don't you, Teddy? You really think we're in charge, don't you?"

"Who is, if we're not?"

"Nick Coletti that's who. He's still calling the shots whether you think so or not."

"You'll never be satisfied, Frank. Even if we took over the town, you'd want the county and then the state."

"I don't think I'll ever have to worry about that with you guys. Why take gold when we can have all the peanuts you want?"

"I take it you're not impressed that they're giving us a thousand a week?"

"You want to know what I think? I think Nick is laughing at us for accepting a thousand a week. With the number of tourists who come to this town on weekends, he's making more than a thousand dollars an hour. I don't even think we've hurt his pride, much less his bank account."

"You're too greedy and ambitious, Frank."

"You want to know what else I think?"

"You're full of depressing thoughts tonight, aren't you? Don't you have anything nice to say?"

"All right," said Frank. "I think you did a damn fine job setting up the room and planning the meeting with them, but we should have told them right then to get the hell out of our town."

"What if they had said no?"

"Then we kick them out?"

"Why get into a fight with them when they'll leave willingly when the time is right?"

"You're supposed to be the military genius, Teddy. It seems like you would welcome a good, knock-down, drag 'em out brawl. What we're doing is no way to run a war."

"There's all kinds of wars, Frank. I want this one to be bloodless."

"Not if I can help it," Frank said and stood up.

"Where you going?"

"To the john, if it's all right with you."

As Frank stomped away, Teddy shook his head in disgust. "What's wrong with him now?" Janet asked.

"Nothing that conquering the world wouldn't cure."

"He wouldn't be satisfied with that," said Janet. "There would still be the universe."

Teddy chuckled and nodded in agreement. Two very cute black girls approached the table cautiously while waiting anxiously for Teddy to look in their direction. Once he did and smiled, the girls were knocking each other over to claim the seat closest to him. Eileen won the race and Marcia had to settle for second best.

"You chicks having fun tonight?"

"Uh huh, but we'd have a lot more fun if you'd dance with us."

"I'd love to, but I have some business going on right now. You understand, don't you?"

"We do, but we just want you to know we'd do anything in the world for you."

"Doggone real," Marcia sighed.

"I know you would, my beautiful, devoted little waifs."

The girls giggled, and Eileen said, "You talk kind of funny, but we love it."

"Of course, you do. But if you're truly sincere, you'll meet me up on Parade Hill Park right after the dance."

"Do you mean it?"

"The only way to find out is to go up there and wait."

"We'll be there!" Marcia assured him as the two girls rushed happily out onto the dance floor.

"You should be ashamed of yourself, Teddy," Janet said while both she and her date were laughing.

"Well, dammit, someone has got to take the responsibility for keeping the beautiful women of the world happy. It's a thankless job, but someone has to do it."

"Sure, Teddy," said Janet. "Oh, by the way, did you hear about the security and intelligence squad? Some of them are branding themselves by burning the initials 'CS' into their lower forearms. Shades of the Nazi SS, isn't it?"

"I do believe you've been reading Mark Jansen's column, Janet."

She laughed and said, "It does sound like something he'd say, doesn't it?"

"YOU YOU YOU," a love ballad sung originally by the Ames Brothers, was being played by the band from Albany. Junie Sando and Mary Granelli came dancing by to ask Teddy what happened to Frank. "He'll be back," said Teddy. "If you see Butch and Augie, send them to me."

"Got ya," Junie said and danced away with Mary in his arms.

Nick Coletti's new Apache Casino was not only operating again, but was doing a considerable amount of business for a Tuesday evening, mainly because it was the night before the Fourth of July and no one was concerned about the time. Nick was all smiles of relief as he sat in the dining area with his son, Tony, Lido, Nappy, and Bummer. Nick had clamped the lid on Tony, made him quit his job at the flower shop and was keeping close tabs on the youth's whereabouts twenty-four hours a day. He didn't realize, of course, that he was playing right into Center Street's hands because Junie Sando had now placed Tony on special assignment to report on all of Nick's activities. One of the waitresses came by and told Lido there was a phone call for him in the office. "For me? Who is it?"

"They didn't say."

"Maybe it's your motha'," Nappy kidded him.

"Maybe it's yours," Lido shot back, and they all laughed.

Looking out over the activity of the casino, Nick said, "Now this really makes me happy. This is the way things should be."

"It should make the Don happy, too," said Nappy.

"It will, it will."

"What about the payments," Bummer asked. "How we gonna' git' it down there?"

Still smiling, Nick said, "I talked to the Don this afternoon, and everything is going to be just fine. He's sending a couple of his boys to pick it up tomorrow."

"That's good," Nappy said.

Nick gave Tony a hug then and said, "Everything's going to be A-okay. Right, son?"

"Right, Dad."

When Junie and Mary joined Teddy at his table, Junie asked again where Frank was.

"Keep your shirt on," said Teddy. "There he is now talking to Helene Mulzer and Cindy Wells."

The Albany band stopped playing, and the drummer was booming a continuous two-beat on the bass drum. Suddenly the throng, being led by Augie Sando in one section and Butch Charles in another, began to chant, "Junie, Junie, Junie!"

Taken completely by surprise, Junie turned to Teddy and said, "Is this your doing?"

"Never mind all that. Go up and talk to them."

As Junie made his way to the bandstand, the teenagers continued to shout his name and clap.

"You just love this, don't you, Teddy," Frank Borzak said as he took the seat next to him.

"You'd better believe it."

"You're wasting a lot of time and energy on him."

"I've got bigger plans than this, Frank."

"I know you do, but it's a waste. He's too soft, too nice. Nice guys finish last, or die young."

"Would you rather it be you up there?"

"I would serve your purpose better than he's going to."

"Now why do I find that hard to believe?"

"Because you don't want to believe it."

"You might be right."

"And what about you," Frank asked. "How can you be so damn happy with second place?"

"Second place looks terrific when there's a Judas running around and a crucifixion is pending."

Frank didn't like that remark and glared at Teddy, who waved his hand and said, "Look at all this, Frank. It's magnificent. Look at the way they love him. They'd die for him. And everyone you see here will be of voting age in six years or less. And if he can do this in Hudson, he can do it all over the state and the country."

"You're wasting your time. He won't be able to do it for you, Teddy."

Teddy looked over at Frank and said, "I'll take my chances, and I'd advise you to think carefully about your loyalties, my friend."

Junie was now up on the bandstand holding up his hands to

quiet the throng. "We've got a few nice surprises for you, but first I've got some news you're really going to like. As you all know, we've been paying you a dollar an hour. As of tomorrow morning the minimum pay scale will be two dollars an hour."

The teenagers all yelled their approval. Junie quieted them down again and continued, "I know it's not going to make any of you rich, but it sure helps, doesn't it?"

The crowd cheered again.

"I got a question," Johnny Capp yelled up.

"What is it, Johnny?"

While laughing, Johnny said, "I want to know when we're going to get another raise."

"When you do some work," Junie answered.

"Oh, no!" cried Dominic Gambino. "Now we'll never get another raise."

The crowd went wild with laughter.

"All right, all right," Junie called out. "There aren't any spies in here tonight, are there?"

"No spies," Kevin Boone yelled. "A lot of ticks, fleas and flies, but no spies."

When the crowd started laughing again, Junie raised his hands to hush them. After taking his time to look caringly at the faces in the crowd, Junie stated, "I cannot begin to tell you how very, very proud I am of each and every one of you, and you should be just as proud of yourselves. They said we couldn't do it. They doubted every thought, word and deed that we had in mind, and we have proven them wrong. We are not a group of silly kids. We are not a bunch of hoodlums. We don't threaten anybody. We haven't killed anyone. You don't mess with us, and we sure won't mess with you. We just want to be left alone. We don't tell you how to run your life, so don't waste your time trying to guide us. We know what we want and what we are. We are, each and every one of us, an individual. Before we are anything else, we are individuals. Don't bother to try to use any negative stereotypes on any of us as to race, color, or creed because we will prove you wrong every time. We are first and foremost men and women. We are Americans. We are New Yorkers. We are Hudsonians. But most of all, we are individuals...and we are smart enough and strong enough and free to do any damn thing we please!"

The crowd started to cheer and scream so loudly the noise echoed out all across the city of Hudson. After giving them time to quiet down, Junie continued solemnly, "We are brothers and sisters. We are family and friends. And we are Love. We are married, and we will remain together until death do us part. The three most important things in your life should be your family, your religion and Center Street...but not necessarily in that order."

Junie and the crowd laughed. Taking the time again to look out at all of the young faces, Junie said, "I love you all so much. I love every one of you; I swear I do. There isn't anything I wouldn't do for you." He took the time to look over at Mary, who, like many of the other teenagers, had tears in her eyes. When Junie raised his hands and yelled, "We are!" the entire hall echoed with "WE ARE!"

"We are one!"

"WE ARE ONE!"

"All right. Is everybody having a good time?"

"YES!"

"Lights. Drum roll."

The house lights dimmed, and the drummer started a steady down beat. When the room was dark, a curtain in the rear of the bandstand parted and a six-foot wide, red, white and blue neon sign lit up that read: "CENTER STREET." The cheering became so loud it was deafening. Junie took the microphone and began to scream, "We are!"

At first no one could hear him. When he screamed it again, they heard it and echoed, "WE ARE!"

"We are!"

"WE ARE!"

"We are one!"

"WE ARE ONE!"

"We are invincible!"

"WE ARE INVINCIBLE!"

"We are!"

"WE ARE!"

"Center Street!"

"CENTER STREET, CENTER STREET, CENTER STREET..."

As the horde continued to chant and stomp and applaud, Frank leaned over to Teddy and said, "You guys finally did it, didn't you?"

"Did what?"

"You've finally made it a Center Street project."

"It's always been a Center Street project from the first moment you talked to us."

"This was my idea!" Frank yelled and stood up.

"Go with us, Frank. Don't turn against us now!"

"This isn't what it was supposed to be."

"Look at it, Frank. It can be yours as well as ours."

"It's his, Teddy. It's Junie's. Not yours or theirs or mine. It's his!"

When Frank turned to leave, Teddy yelled, "Where are you going?"

"Home!" Frank yelled back and started for the door.

"BRUCE!" Teddy shouted to his brother who was at the other end of the table. "See that Frank goes straight home."

"Got ya."

After the party, Teddy was walking downtown alone. Marty was waiting for him at the corner of Second Street. Marty asked if he could have a word.

"Sure, as long as you don't mind walking with me down to Parade Hill Park."

Once they started, Marty confessed that he, with Janet and Frank, had paid a visit to the training camp out in the claybanks that morning. "Frank and Janet were more than pleased with what they saw, but in all honesty, Teddy, I was appalled and not just a tiny bit frightened."

"Why?"

"Why!? Teddy, they're learning how to slit throats, strangle, poison people, and bomb houses."

"So?"

"Those are not conventional war maneuvers."

"We're not fighting a conventional war."

"We're not fighting a war at all!"

"Not yet," Teddy said.

"Let me ask you a question. Where will we go and what will we do if the unthinkable were to happen?"

"The unthinkable? What do you mean?"

"Teddy...think. You've studied history. How do heroes become martyrs?"

"How?" Teddy asked innocently.

"By dying for their cause."

"Junie's not going to die."

"I know, but what if he should?"

"He can't die. I mean, if he did..."

"Exactly."

"What are you getting at, Marty?"

"We have to do something to break the machinery down before it goes on a reckless, murdering rampage. Those Warriors are brainwashed. They're robots. More than that, you have them intoxicated with the idea of war. Not only war, but of killing should something happen to Junie."

"But I thought that's what we wanted...without the violence, of course."

"Teddy, don't be naive. Sooner or later some form of violence is sure to come. You know that. You've created the machine, and it's up to you to break it down. Frank lives for it, Janet would welcome it. Junie is even more naive than you because he doesn't know, like you and I, what the Warriors can and will do."

"He knows."

"Does he? I don't think so. All he knows is that you have them prepared, not that you've trained them to be assassins."

"During World War Two the O.S.S. made assassinations part of war."

"Teddy, this is little, jerkwater Hudson, New York, not Nazi Germany during World War Two. You're going to want to be able to keep control of them in case of an emergency. But that mob I saw today is ready for one thing and one thing only...murder. They should be learning defensive measures, not aggression. After all, they're still kids, you know?"

"Some of them are in their twenties."

"That is totally irrelevant. Do you agree with me or not?"

"Not necessarily, but you do make a good point. All right, starting tomorrow, first thing, we'll go back to the basics. It won't take long."

Marty exhaled a deep sigh and said, "Let's hope there's still time. God knows, there better be."

16

Teddy: "Tuck Ryan was a great little guy. Brave, fragile, loyal and defenseless as a daisy. There were many reasons for hating Nick and the Mob, but none more than for what they did to Tuck. Poor Tuck. He had a little girl. Debbie. She had polio. His wife Kathy was pregnant with their second child. We gave her a batch of money and a car, and like so many other people, she disappeared in the night."

The Fourth of July, 1959, was destined to be a red, white and blue day. The sun rose promptly at five-thirteen, awoke the birds, dried the moisture that had gathered on the leaves, and then confronted a mammoth, dark gray layer of clouds that came thundering in from the west. Humbled, the sun smiled brightly one last time, then relented and disappeared, leaving the earth in relative darkness.

So quiet, so light, it was the kind of morning rain that one can barely feel. It was a dainty rain, a faint, warm, elegant, lacy type of drizzle that falls like drops of dew in slow motion against cotton. At once it could relieve the cares of the day, the despairs of the moment and inspire lovers to take a stroll.

Strolling among the desolate claybanks were four men. Three were dressed in suits. The fourth, his hands tied behind him, his head battered and bloody, was wearing only blue slacks and a white t-shirt.

When Tuck Ryan saw his impending grave, he stopped and was shoved forward by Lido Sandrelli. As Tuck reached the open grave, he stood shivering, not from the chill of rain, but from fear. From fright, and death.

"You got anything to say, Tuck?" Lido asked.

"Who told you about me?"

"A little bird. One of your little friends sang to me last night."

"The Streeters wouldn't tell you."

"They wouldn't, huh? Then how did we find out, and why are you here? Hah. What's your last words, Tuck?"

Catching his breath, Tuck took a moment and then began, "I want to say that I love my wife, my kids and especially my mother. And I want her to forgive me for being a coward all my life. But I ain't gonna' die no coward. You guys ain't nothin' but a bunch of lousy punks! And I pray to God the Streeters get you. I know they will; I just hope they make you suffer."

"You through?" Lido asked.

"Yes, and so are you."

Lido shoved Tuck down to his knees and placed a snubnosed .38 at the base of his skull and waited for him to plead for his life. Tuck, keeping his promise not to die a coward, bit his bottom lip until the blood trickled down his chin and dripped onto his t-shirt. The first shot was muffled, as were the second and third, with the sounds echoing off and around the claybanks as Tuck tumbled forward. Lido emptied the gun into the body and then threw it into the grave to be buried with the corpse.

The rain stopped at 8:54 a.m., leaving the streets shining and clean as the sun began to fight its way through the myriad of clouds. Red, white and blue flags were being displayed on every building and were wrapped around telephone poles along Hudson's main street. Marching bands from all over the state created a jaunting cacophony of sounds as they tuned up on Parade Hill. The local VIPs and dignitaries were certain to be on the reviewing stand in front of City Hall every Fourth of July. Mayor Cameron Brown, serving his third term and going for a fourth in November, arranged to be the only speaker. He took this golden opportunity to boast of his administration and to blast his opponents. While trumpeting the glories of Hudson, he gave a tremendous plug to Center Street by saying, "And how about those great teenagers of ours bringing peace at long last to our streets and finding jobs and helping each other in a spirit that is so American it literally tugs at my heartstrings." Sensing the crowd was restless, the mayor cut his speech short and sent word for the parade to begin.

The Grenadiers from the Mohawk Valley, dressed in bright white uniforms with thin red trimming and gold helmets with high blue plumes, were everyone's favorite. Many children and grown-ups followed them from one end of the parade route to the other. Some of the other bands, such as the Elks from Schenectady, the American Legion of Catskill, and the Cadets of Syracuse, were exciting to hear and very worth watching, but none compared to the Grenadiers.

Center Street didn't have a band, but they did have red, white and blue alerts. The red alert was a call for their security and intelligence squad to assemble at the warehouse, prepare for battle and proceed immediately to the point of conflict. The white alert was for all soldiers not on special assignments. And the blue alert was for everyone available to rush to the point of encounter.

The parade was nearing its end when the red, white and blue alerts went out for the Hudson train station. The S&I squad arrived first after being summoned there by the three boys who were on guard. Two men, obviously Don Carlucci's hoods, had arrived. The first thing to be done by the guards was to call it in and then cut the telephone wires.

The two thugs knew something was amiss when both station phone booths were out of order. The Don had warned them, and they were no less worried when the S&I squad rushed in, stood back against the walls of the station and absolutely refused to look at them. When one of the men walked over to the ticket window, it was slammed shut. As he turned, he saw that the room, forty by fifty-five feet, was filling with more teenage boys who also didn't look at the hoods.

"What do you kids want?" the larger one shouted.

Boris Robanski turned to them and said politely, "We are here for your protection, sir."

"We don't need you. Clear out!"

Suddenly, at least thirty teenagers of all sizes and shapes rushed in through the front and back doors, crowded themselves into the room, stopped suddenly and refused to look at the men.

Now the hoods were actually scared and became even more so when Skippy McDonald, Moe Garnett, Johnny Capp, Bruce West and Dominic Gambino started to move toward them with their backs turned. And then suddenly all five boys spun around pointing handguns.

"Strip them!" Boris ordered, and the men were quickly relieved of their weapons.

The kids cleared a path so Boris could walk to the ticket window. He knocked three times, and the clerk opened up.

"What time is the next train to New York City?"

"It's due in about fourteen minutes."

"Is it on time?"

"Yes."

Boris walked over to the men. "Your train back to the city is due in fourteen minutes. Get on it and tell Don Carlucci the next time he sends any men up here, they're going to be delivered C.O.D. and D.O.A. If he thinks we're kidding, tell him to try it."

Boris turned and snapped his fingers, and everyone except the S&I squad quickly departed from the station.

A call came over the walkie-talkies that there was serious trouble at the warehouse. Junie Sando drove there as quickly as he could. Rushing up the stairs he was met by Marty Politzsky, Frank Borzak and Jeri-Mae Charles, Butch's sister.

"What is it?"

"Tell him, Jeri," Frank said.

"I think they killed Tuck."

"What happened?"

"When he didn't show up at the pool hall this morning, I called his house. The line was busy. I put in an emergency call and the operator said the phone was off the hook. So I went over there and found Mrs. Ryan crying and packing to leave town. She said Lido, Nappy and Bummer came before sunrise and took Tuck away. She hasn't heard from him since."

"Maybe they're just holding him," Marty offered.

"Holding him, my ass," said Frank. "They're holding him like they're still holding Danny Tiano."

"Poor Tuck," said Jeri-Mae.

"We've got to get them, Junie!" Frank warned. "They've killed Tuck, and they're going to start hitting us one by one."

"We're teenagers," Marty cried. "They won't touch us!"

"Bullshit, Marty!" Frank shouted. "Now is the time, Junie."

"I'm going to call him." Junie went into the main office, followed by the others.

"Why are you going to call Nick? You know damn well he ordered it!"

"I don't believe it," Junie said and dialed.

"Apache."

"Let me speak to Nick Coletti."

"Just a minute."

"You're going to let him talk his way out of it!" Frank warned.

"Hello," Nick said, coming to the phone.

"You hit Tuck Ryan. Why?"

Nick was silent.

"I'm talking to you, asshole! Why did you hit Tuck?"

"Oh, God," Nick barely uttered. "My men haven't reported in yet. I don't know anything about it."

"You expect me to believe that?"

"I swear to God on my mother's grave, may she rot in hell if I knew anything about it."

"I don't believe you."

"You tell me what you want me to do to prove it, and I will. To prove it to you, or make it up to you."

"How can you make it up to me? Can you dig Tuck up and bring him back to life?"

"Was he working for you?"

"Yes!" Junie yelled. "But he was harmless, and you know it."

After a pause, Nick said, "I know, and I wouldn't have touched him. I'll make it up to you. I'll get rid of Lido Sandrelli, if that's what you want."

"I'll let you know what I want, and you goddamn sure better do it!"

"I will. I swear I will. You have my word on it. What's your name, kid?" Nick asked kindly.

"What difference does it make? You're up against an entire army that would just as soon kill you as spit on you."

"I know. And if it's any consolation to you, I'm scared shitless. What's your name, kid? You can trust me."

After hesitating, Junie replied proudly, "Junie. Junie Sando."

"Are you Frederico Sandolini's oldest son?"

"Yes, I am."

129

"I've noticed you. I see you at Sunday Mass. You're a very sharp young man. Junie, let me make a suggestion. I want to work with you. We'll keep it just between the two of us. Let's you and me stop this thing from blowing up, okay? We can do it. You don't want that and neither do I."

Junie felt that Nick was being sincere but he could not forget, nor could he erase, the fact that Nick was directly responsible not only for the death of Tuck, but especially for the murder of Danny Tiano.

"Okay?" Nick asked.

"We'll see."

"Talk to me, Junie. Call me. Work with me. It could...it could possibly keep us both alive."

"I don't like you, Nick."

"I know, I understand, but I think this thing is about to go beyond whether we like each other or not. I think you know what I mean."

It was a blue and purple sunset that evening. The sky had turned red at first, and then dozens of shimmering white rays streamed down from behind the pillows of clouds that towered over the horizon. The blue-gray Hudson river lay peaceful as if frozen in time. Having been stung by the stark reality of Tuck Ryan's murder, the teenagers of Hudson were subdued. A few, but just a few, quit Center Street, "chickened out" and defected back to their parents. One sixteen-year-old, with tears running down his cheeks while quivering in fear, pleaded with Junie Sando to understand. He did, of course, and the boy went scampering home. But the vast majority of the members, though filled with trepidation, held fast. The warehouse, usually a hubbub of activity, was all but still. Two soldiers stood guard at the front door, and a few kids sat solemnly listening to the juke box.

Now that all the gangs in the city had become one, the Black Leopards were often seen in the north end of Parade Hill Park. Having drawn morning assignments, the boys were free for the afternoon. A kid, originally from Georgia, by the name of Boots Griffin was doing the talking, and most of it was directed at the leader of the Leopards, Louis MacKey. "I'm tellin' ya, man, we ain't got no business in this shit now."

"What do you want us to do, Boots?" Louis asked calmly.

"Git out of it! Quit Center Street. Tell Junie and Teddy to shove it."

Louis glanced at Boots and then at the other four members who were sitting quietly on the grass.

"They usin' us, Louis," Boots continued. "When Teddy West split with us, he took only his brothers, the Charles family and the Hines family. I bet there wasn't even ten Leopards in Center Street. Teddy wanted to take our best man, Moe Garnett, but Moe had sense enough to stick with you. Now he's doin' most of their dirty work for them. I ain't sayin' it was wrong for us. Hell, we made some good poke, but the shit's about to hit the fan with them shootin' each otha. You let them catch just one of us mixed up in the shit, and they gonna' start shootin' at us. Now, all you got to do, Louis, is tell Junie we pullin' out. It's been fun, but the fun's over and we gone."

Louis looked again at the other boys and asked, "What do you guys think?"

"We're with you, Louis."

"All the way."

"Boots got a point, but you're the boss, Louis."

"That's right."

Louis took a deep breath, gave it some thought and began, "Teddy West came to me like a man. Explained it to me, told me what the gig was and gave me a choice. I told him I believe in him. I gave him my word. I ain't gonna' say I ain't scared, but I'll be damned if I'm gonna go back on my word. But you guys ain't gotta' stay. I swear there ain't gonna' be no hard feelings, but my word is my bond."

"But why should we stay in this shit, Louis?" Boots asked. "It ain't our fight."

Louis lowered his head and then raised it looking directly at Boots. "Maybe it ain't our fight, but it's our town. For betta' or worse, and it sure ain't much, but it's the only town we got."

Boots stared at Louis for a moment, cursed under his breath, got up, walked over to the fence and looked out over the peaceful Hudson River as the high tide began to find its way up to the shore and under the pier where the old wooden ferry boat to Coxsackie would dock and take passengers across the river.

There was a hardy Bing cherry tree in back of the house on Union Street that the family protected like a relative. During the season, its large, sweet black balls of fruit would flourish and cause the branches to strain and bend to the ground until they were picked, pitted and cooked in one of Mrs. Maggie Boone's famous favorite pies. Walking out into the backyard, Harold Boone, Kevin and Burt's father, wondered why the boys weren't out celebrating the Fourth of July. He also wanted to know why they weren't playing any sports that summer.

"We want to work this summer, Pop," Kevin answered simply.

"All work and no play makes Jack a dull boy."

Kevin and Burt looked at each other, and Kevin said, "All play and no work is much worse. And seeing that we've been playing most of our lives, we like the change."

"All right, but we're all going over to your aunt Sarah's. Why don't you come and go with us?"

"We're a little worn out from working so much, Pop. We'll go with you next week, okay?"

Disappointed, Harold shrugged and said, "Suit yourselves."

After their father was gone, Burt turned to Kevin and said, "Suppose we're asked to kill?"

"We won't be asked to kill."

"How do you know?"

"Junie will figure out a way."

"He didn't figure out a way to save Tuck Ryan."

"Don't worry about it."

"Suppose they kill Junie, too?"

Kevin hesitated and then answered, "Then that's it, isn't it?"

When Burt was about to say something else, Kevin took him by the wrist and turned it over to reveal the scorched CS tattoo that the Warriors had proudly endured. "Do you remember the vow you took when you accepted this? You swore you would follow orders to the death."

"I know, but I really didn't think it would go this far."

"It's what we've been training for."

"I know," Burt said again and frowned.

Kevin punched him playfully in the shoulder and said, "You'll do okay."

"Ain't you scared?"

"No. Because Center Street is invincible...and we are Center Street."

"I don't even know what invincible means."

Kevin chuckled while saying, "You'll find out."

Though they had finished eating dinner, the kitchen still smelled of boiled ham and potatoes. Bobby and Bruce West sat staring at Teddy, who broke the silence with, "I told Junie it could happen. I told him. They all thought it was going to be a joyride." Teddy stopped and frowned.

"I still don't believe they'll start killing us," Bobby offered.

"It doesn't matter," said Teddy. "Danny Tiano was a traitor, and he was one of their own, but Tuck Ryan was ours. The Center Street eternal Motto is that we take care of our own. We have to strike back."

"You want us to hit one of them?" Bruce asked.

"No. But we've got to make them pay somehow."

"How about telling them to pay us three thousand a week?" Bobby suggested.

"I don't know," said Teddy, and then grimacing he said, "Damn! They killed Tuck. They actually murdered him. How can they do that? Just kill somebody like that?"

"They're animals," Bruce offered.

"God knows I didn't want any part of this," Teddy sighed. "I told Junie that, I warned him."

"They won't touch us," Bruce tried to reassure him. "They hit one kid from Center Street, and they'll all go straight to hell."

Teddy looked over at his older brother, was concerned for him, touched his arm and said, "I've got to think this out. I'll be in my room if anybody calls."

Millie West, a durable, loving, hard-working woman, had been standing in the hallway listening to the boys' conversation. She entered the room now and said, "Remember what I always told you two...you look out for Teddy. I don't give a damn about your organization or anything else. You look out for your baby brother. You hear me?"

"Yes, Mother," the two older boys answered.

Millie entered Teddy's bedroom to find him lying face down on the bed. Sitting next to him, she began to rub his back.

After a moment, Teddy leaned up on his elbow and said, "What did I do wrong, Mom?"

"It's not your fault, Teddy. None of what went wrong is your fault. You've always done the right thing, and you always will. People just don't listen to you sometimes, but it's not your fault. You'll learn a lesson from this. Don't ever count on other people to do the things you can do yourself. You'll always do it right. You hear me?"

"Yes, Mother."

"You all right now?" Millie asked.

"I didn't want any part of this."

"Then you shouldn't have got into it."

"I know, but I thought I could keep it peaceful."

"There ain't no peace in the heart of a mad dog, Teddy, and mad dogs is what you're dealing with."

After a pause, Teddy said, "They shoot mad dogs, don't they, Mother?"

Millie patted his back and said, "Yes, they do. Every one of them." Rising then, she left Teddy's room. Entering the kitchen she stopped to look at Bruce and Bobby.

"Don't worry, Mom, we'll take care of him," Bruce assured her.

"You'd better," said Millie. "Or you're no sons of mine."

Junie Sando and Mary Granelli had driven out to the rolling hills overlooking the mile-long Rip Van Winkle Bridge to watch the sun set in back of the Catskill Mountains. The sun was gone now, and a few stars had begun to appear. Knowing the pain Junie was feeling, Mary cuddled close to him.

"Oh, wow!" Junie groaned. "We've got to clean it up."

"Clean what up?"

"The town. If we keep it, we'll have to do what they did today. We've got to just run them out and clean up the damn place. We can't run those operations, not for one minute."

Mary smiled.

"I can't believe we even thought of doing anything else," Junie continued. "We have to clean it up. We'll start first thing in the morning."

"Do you feel better now?" Mary asked.

"Yes. Yes, I do."

"Is it all settled?"

Knowing what she was getting at, Junie nodded that it was settled.

"Good," said Mary. "And now would you mind concentrating on me a little?"

Taking her into his arms Junie kissed her fully on the lips. It was a hot night and, for many reasons, Mary pulled her skirt up to her waist, revealing her long, shapely, smooth legs, especially that mellow softness of the inner thigh. Junie's hand was there now, grasping, feeling and moving upward. Soon he touched the silk of her panties and felt the warmth there. As if angry, but not, Mary grabbed and wrestled with Junie, hugging him as if she wanted to pull him bodily inside of her. They were both frantically grabbing at each other, moaning, kissing; and Junie's fingers slipped up under the edge of her panties. They ceased grabbing. Then they merely held each other.

"Oh, Junie, please..." Mary said without being able to complete the sentence.

"I know, I know," he said and held her close.

"Junie?"

"Yes."

"I don't want to make love in the car tonight. Please not tonight."

"Okay. Where do you want to go?"

"I don't know. In a bed somewhere."

"Jack Losse's using the warehouse apartment."

"We could go to the Pine Tree Motel," Mary suggested.

"Why not?

It was a plain, flat, elongated building that sat on a deserted stretch of highway 9H. It consisted of an office and a line of ten rooms with parking alcoves. It was not a place to hide, and quite often on weekends snoopers would drive out late at night to see if they could catch someone cheating. The room, like the motel, was plain with a double bed, dresser, chair, small bathroom and tub, a framed cardboard landscape on the wall, and an end table with a lamp. It was the type of room to be used for only two things, either sleeping or making love.

Mary and Junie sat silently on opposite sides of the bed while undressing. When they were both nude, they acted almost as if it was their first time together, or their last. Shyly, childishly, they covered themselves before turning. Once their eyes met, their love flowed as they moved to each other and embraced.

At nineteen Mary had perfect breasts. They were round, large and firm. Junie loved to take them lightly in his hands and bury his face in them, licking the nipples until they hardened and protruded.

Finding her lips again, Junie kissed her with his eyes closed to savor the moment. Mary always left her eyes open, uncertain as she still was that Junie was really hers. She knew he was, but somehow it was still too good to be true. So she would watch him as they kissed, and quite often it would bring tears to her eyes as it did now.

As they continued to kiss, she maneuvered him onto his back so she could crawl on top of him. And just as she prepared to let him slip into her, Junie said, "Hold it." He got up, lifted his pants from the floor, searched his wallet and said, "Ohh, no!"

"What's wrong?"

"I don't have a Trojan."

They looked at each other then, and Mary merely held out her hand for Junie to come to her.

"But I don't have a rubber, Mary."

Feeling the night-time chill, Mary crawled under the sheet and bedspread and again reached for Junie. Getting in beside her, Junie warned that she might get pregnant if they didn't use protection.

Still, without a word, Mary took him into her arms.

"What if you get pregnant?"

Mary silenced him with a kiss. With another and another. She could feel him from head to toe now, and as she spread her legs, Junie moved on top of her, and they melted into each other.

17

Teddy: "Oh, God, how I wish we could have stopped it right then, or never begun it at all. Colonel George S. Patton the Third was once heard to say, 'I do like to see the arms and legs fly.' Well, I don't and I didn't. How ridiculous we all were to think it would simply go away. Why...why didn't one of us say, 'Hey, we've made our point. Let's quit while we're ahead.' But no..."

Tireless Jeff Gershon had been following Mark Jansen for the last three days. After watching Mark being rejected by all of the authorities in the Capitol, Jeff decided to report back to Center Street at noon on July the Fifth.

"From what I could hear and see, Mark's getting the same runaround up there he did here. Of course, it was over the holiday but they were definitely annoyed with him. The last time I saw him this morning he was sitting in the lobby of the F.B.I. building waiting to talk to anybody who would listen to him. They told him they would call the Hudson police chief. Believe me, they'll be fed up with him in no time at all."

"Good job, Jeff," said Junie. "Go home and get some rest and check in with us later."

After Jeff was gone, Junie, who was feeling good for numerous reasons, smiled as he studied the board members, Teddy, Frank, Marty, Janet, Augie and Butch.

"I've called you here today because I've come to a decision."

Frank knew immediately what it was and said, "I would like to say something if you don't mind."

"It's not going to do any good, Frank. My mind is made up."

"But we all started this thing together!"

"Frank," Teddy began, "General Rommel said, 'If one knows how to begin a war, one had better know how to end it.'"

"And we're ending it," said Junie. "We're going to clean up the town."

"Thank God," Marty sighed. Janet, Teddy and Butch all smiled in relief.

"We don't want to become what they are," Junie continued. "We don't want to have to kill people like Tuck Ryan. We don't want to kill anybody."

"They started it."

"That's no reason for us to do it, Frank."

"But it is!"

"I agree with Frank," Augie announced.

"Well, well, well," Janet said. "Witness the most unholy and un-healthy alliance ever formed. How long have you two been break-ing bread?"

"We ain't been breakin' no bread," Augie snapped.

"If we don't take it, someone else will," Frank warned. "This town is a perfect setup for this type of thing. And the people of Hudson wouldn't have it any other way."

"But we will," said Marty. "We won't allow it to happen ever again."

"That's big talk, Marty," said Augie. "But you can be bumped off, too, you know?"

"By who, Augie? You?"

"If Center Street asked me to, I would do it."

"Center Street is asking you to help clean up the town. Why can't you do that?"

"Because Frank's right. If we don't take it, somebody else will."

"How do you know?"

"How do you know they won't?"

"Because the minute anyone tries, we'll start harassing them."

"You think that's going to work every time, Marty?" Frank asked.

"Nick Coletti just happened to be the cautious man at the right time. Imagine what would have happened to us if Lido Sandrelli had been in charge instead of Nick."

"It might not have been easy, but we still would have done it," said Junie.

"Don't be so sure."

"Frank's right," Augie said. "We shouldn't just throw it away so easy."

"We don't want to grow up to be hoodlums, Augie."

"What makes you think you're not!" Frank said, and everyone fell silent. They all stared at him, but no one more intensely than Junie Sando.

"You think so, huh, Frank?"

"Can you prove to me that you're not?"

"Why does he have to?" Marty asked.

"We're all hoodlums, otherwise we couldn't have done what we did," Frank explained. "Nick and his bunch are gutter rats, and we had to get right down in the gutter with them. We can't all of a sudden be something we're not. We're just a bunch of small-town squares with nowhere to go and nothing to do but what our town offers. And right now it offers what Nick Coletti has. Do we just throw away the greatest opportunity we'll ever have, or do we keep it and get rich?"

There was a pause, and then Marty spoke softly, "We throw it away, Frank."

"Junie?"

"Tomorrow morning, Frank, we start harassing them again until they leave."

"It won't work, Junie. They killed Tuck Ryan, and they'll start killing us if we start harassing them again."

"Nick Coletti won't kill us," Janet stated.

"Maybe not, but Lido will."

"If he does," said Junie, "then I will take care of Lido personally. Now you all know what to do. The organization will continue to function as it is, but with a different purpose in mind...to disrupt and destroy Nick Coletti's operations. Let's get on it. I'll go give Jack Losse the bad news. He's going to have to give up all this good living and go back to hustling penny-ante games."

As Junie was getting up to depart, Frank and Augie went into a private huddle.

"Well," said Marty, "let's get it over with."

Marty and Janet got up to leave.

When Frank and Augie stood, Teddy said, "Where are you going, Frank?"

"I've got work to do."

"I can't think of anything you're supposed to do. Junie didn't give you any orders."

Augie left the room.

"Things are different now, Teddy."

"Sit down, Frank. I've got some serious thinking to do, and you're my main inspiration."

Nick Coletti was glad that the night and morning had passed without a reaction from the Streeters over the death of Tuck Ryan. He had expected, in the least, some harassment but none had come, so he was quite relieved. He knew they could still do something, if they chose. Perhaps Lido and the men were right: this act would keep them in line. Nick entered the Apache Casino and was welcomed by some of the workers and a few of the regular gamblers. He was beginning to feel that things would be running smoothly again. He wanted this more than anything else in the world, even at the cost of making a deal with the Streeters. But all of this was shattered as he entered the office and found Lido and Nappy loading shells into their sawed-off, pump-action Winchester M12 shotguns. Nick was afraid to ask. Lido finished loading his weapon, glanced over at Nick and shrugged.

"What is it now?" Nick asked.

"I just got a phone call," Lido explained. "They haven't learned yet. They've got that card shark Jack Losse staying over at their warehouse."

"So what?"

"Nick, don't be stupid. They're planning on taking over your operations, and he's going to run the casinos for them...if we let him."

"I want to give this some thought," Nick said, stalling for time.

"Nick," Lido said softly, "I'm sorry, but I talked to the Don this morning. He said it's okay for me to handle this my way."

"But everything's going to be okay now," Nick said. "We don't have to do this, Lido. Nappy?!"

"It's the only way, boss," said Nappy. "You're still in charge, but we got to do this."

"Just relax, boss," said Bummer. "We'll have this over with in no time at all. Just wait here and give us fifteen or twenty minutes, and all your problems will be solved."

As the three men started for the door, Nick chuckled sarcastically and asked, "Do we all want to die? Is that what we're going after? They've got an Army!"

"Hey, boss," Nappy said, "take it easy. They're just kids."

"They're kids, boss," Bummer added. "We'll take care of 'um and we'll be back in no time."

"There's no other way," Lido said. "This is it."

"No matter what happens?"

"No matter what happens," Lido replied and left the office with Bummer and Nappy. Nick, more concerned and confused than ever, plopped into the office chair to worry and wait.

Lido noticed the boys up on the roof watching them as the three men got into the 1958 Lincoln. Lido and Nappy sat in the back seat, holding the shotguns under raincoats. Bummer got into the driver's seat.

"They're watching us," Bummer said.

"I know," said Lido. "Drive up to Third Street and make a quick turn to the right. Me and Nappy will jump out, and you keep driving. Give us ten minutes to make our way through the gangways to the warehouse, and then you come barrel-assing up the alley to the back door to get us."

"Got you!"

"...so that's the way it is, Jack," Junie was saying to Jack Losse as they sat having drinks in the warehouse apartment. "We've decided to clean it up. Chase them out and tear it all down the second they're gone."

Gazing at his glass of Wild Turkey, Jack smiled and said, "It's been great, and you know what I wish?"

"What?"

"That I was a teenager again so I could be in this thing with you guys."

"Don't be so sure. We haven't done it yet."

"Yes, but you will," said Jack. "It's amazing how good you guys are. You could have used all this energy doing bad things, and you're not. But I guess you're responsible for that. You're the leader."

"I've tried to keep it clean, but Tuck Ryan got killed."

"That wasn't your fault. Sooner or later they always have to kill somebody. Lido is the one you have to worry about. He's bad news."

"I know, and I'm afraid it's going to have to come to a showdown between Lido and me."

"If it does, my money's on you."

When Junie said, "Don't bet the farm," they both laughed.

"I never bet the farm," said Jack.

Lido and Nappy had maneuvered their way through backyards, gangways and over fences and were now at the side of the Center Street warehouse. Peeking out into the alley, they found it empty. They ran to the front door, shoved it open, caught two guards by surprise and pushed them ahead as they went upstairs.

Junie and Jack were coming out of the apartment as Jack was saying, "Kitty and I have become pretty close. I'm going to go over there and see if I can talk her into going with me. I'll come back for my stuff when-" Jack and Junie stopped as they saw Lido and Nappy pointing their shotguns at them. The two guards were lying prone on the floor. Lido looked from Junie to Jack and then his eyes shifted from one to the other and stopped finally on Junie.

"We told you not to take it any further."

Lido then turned to Jack and fired a blast that caught him squarely in the chest lifting him in the air. Lido instantly pumped another shell into the chamber and fired. The second shot splattered Jack against the back wall.

"That's it, kids," Nappy shouted. "You stop where you are."

Lido now turned his attention to Junie, pumped the shotgun, ejecting a spent shell, and leveled the gun at him.

"Let's go, Lido," Nappy said and then turned quickly as Teddy and Frank opened the door to the main office.

"Get back in there!"

Frank pulled Teddy back into the room and slammed the door.

When Bruce and Bobby West came charging up the stairs, Nappy ordered them down on the floor with the guards. As Lido and Junie continued to stare at each other, their eyes locked and even though Junie could feel death only seconds away, a faint smile crossed his lips.

"Let's go, Lido!" Nappy shouted again. "Bummer's waiting."

Softly, heinously, Lido said to Junie, "You're no kid."

"NO, LIDO!" Nappy screamed just as Lido pulled the trigger and hundreds of cold, steel buckshots caught Junie throwing his hands up for protection, but in vain. The pellets shredded Junie's hands and opened up his stomach. A quick action on the pump, a spent shell flew into the air, and Lido fired again. This time the blast hit Junie in the upper right chest and throat and shattered his right jawbone with the force knocking his right eyeball out of its socket as he fell back against the wall and slid to the floor.

Nappy stared at the two corpses, whispered, "Oh my God," and pulled on Lido so they could leave.

The second the men were out of the front door, Bruce ran to the office calling for Teddy. Teddy came out into the hallway and saw Junie lying against the back wall with his intestines exposed, blood running out of his body, and his right eye hanging out on the cheek. Beginning to quiver, Teddy then screamed as he crossed the hall and fell on his knees five yards from Junie. When Johnny Capp and Kevin and Burt Boone came running up the stairs, Frank yelled, "Lock that downstairs door and don't let anybody out of here!"

The three boys stopped at the top of the stairs, saw the bodies, and Burt shouted, "Noooo!"

"Johnny, go lock that damn door!" Johnny awoke, heard Frank and ran back downstairs.

Having heard the gunfire, but afraid to come out of the office, Janet and Marty stepped cautiously now into the hallway. "Jesus H. Christ," Janet moaned as Teddy and Burt and some of the other kids continued to cry out loud. Bruce and Bobby were standing on either side of Teddy now as he remained catatonic while staring at Junie.

Going over to Teddy West, Frank bent down and said, "Lido did it. Lido Sandrelli did it. Do we get that son-of-a- bitch? Do we?"

Marty was there now, sobbing and frightened while knowing what Frank was asking.

"No, Frank!"

Spinning and grabbing Marty by the throat, Frank said, "You keep your fucking mouth out of this, Marty, or I swear to God I'll kill you!"

"Teddy's in charge now."

Speaking softly, Frank said, "Does he look like he's in any shape to take charge?"

"We can't start killing people, Frank."

Frank drew back and hit Marty solidly in the jaw, laying him out cold in the hallway. Turning back to Teddy, who had stopped screaming but was still paralyzed by shock, Frank leaned down to him again and pleaded, "Teddy, Lido did it. Nick and Lido did it. Don't you want those bastards to pay for this? Don't you want them to suffer and die the way Junie just did? Just say 'Yes,' Teddy. Say yes, please, say yes, and I'll fix those bastards, those dogs, those mangy fucking dogs. Say yes, Teddy, please say yes."

"Yes..." Teddy barely uttered, and the word sent a shock wave of power through Frank's entire body.

"Thank you. Thank you, Teddy," Frank whispered and stood. "All right. All right now. Bruce, you and Bobby-"

"No," Bruce said firmly. "We're staying with Teddy."

"Of course, that's good. You two stay here with Teddy, guard the warehouse, and," Frank turned back to Junie, "and see that no one touches him. I want the Warriors...I want all the Warriors to see it."

Walking down the hall, Frank made it known he was now in power. "Let's go!" he shouted at the two guards, and Burt and Kevin Boone. "We've got work to do."

When they got down to the front door, Frank could see that there were a lot of Streeters waiting outside.

"Let only the Warriors in, tell the others to go home and stay by their phones. We'll be in touch. And Johnny, I want every Warrior to go up and take a look at Junie. Then tell them to report to me downstairs."

All but overcome himself, Johnny Capp was unable to speak, so he simply nodded.

The last meeting ever to take place at Center Street began at 2:37 p.m. on July 5, 1959. Janet Hammond, her eyes red and swollen, was still beside herself with grief. She and Frank Borzak were accompanied by Cindy Wells, the tall, brunette leader of the Debs. The three of them took seats up on the bandstand and Janet asked Cindy to speak for her. The Warriors, some unable to hide their weeping, had seen Junie's body and were aware of what was going to be asked of them.

"You will be dividing into squads," Cindy Wells began. "The first squad will apprehend Lido Sandrelli. The Lido squad will be led by Johnny Capp with Moe Garnett and Skippy McDonald."

Burt Boone was so pleased that the three toughest and meanest boys would go after Lido that he began to cry again, this time in joy.

"The second squad, the Nappy Gaudio squad, will be led by Kevin

Boone with Boris Robanski and Dominic Gambino. The Bummer Minghini squad will be Louis MacKey, Burt Boone and Spike Danner. The Nick Coletti squad will be Jeff Gershon, Butch Charles and Stucko McNair. Each squad will have a driver. The drivers will be Boots Griffin, Donald Morrant, Benny Hines and Steve Granowski. The rest of you will be back-up men in case somebody decides to chicken out, or if any of the missions fail you will shoot the hoods on sight. The bodies will be delivered to the claybanks where graves will be prepared and waiting. You will spend the rest of the afternoon planning and preparing for your mission and learning the whereabouts of your targets. All activities will take place under the cover of darkness. Are there any questions?"

"What about the rest of the people who work for Nick?" Jeff Gershon asked.

"They're just flunkies. Harmless flunkies. They'll disappear the minute Nick and the others are missing."

"What exactly do you want done with Lido?" Johnny Capp asked.

After a pause, Cindy said, "If it was my assignment, I wouldn't have to ask. Or maybe you better go upstairs and take another look at Junie."

When there were no more questions, Cindy said, "Frank will speak to you now."

Frank stood and paused, relishing the moment. Speaking softly, he began, "We didn't ask for this. And I, especially, didn't ask for this. But here we are...thrust into a moment of unparalleled destiny. There are those, like our friend Marty Politzsky, who would have us turn the other cheek at what Lido Sandrelli did to Junie. He would like for us to leave it up to the courts to decide. Of course, the chances of one of them going to jail are slim to none. They killed Jack Losse and nobody cares...except us."

Frank stopped and then yelled, "THEY KILLED DANNY! And they killed Tuck Ryan, and nobody's mentioned their names since. Well, I'll be goddamned to hell forever if they're going to kill Junie Sando and laugh it off. Not Junie, they're not. Oh, no." Frank took a moment to regain his control. "I...I loved Junie Sando. We had our differences. Hell, I know I'm not the easiest person in the world to get along with. So we had our differences, but was there ever a nicer, cooler or sweeter guy in this world than Junie? Why Junie? Why not me? I'll tell you why, because he was the best of us. By far the best of us.

"You don't have to worry about getting caught, or Don Carlucci taking revenge on us, or even going to prison. The police are on our side. And don't worry about an investigation, or some B.C.I. or F.B.I. man coming down from Albany. Lido and the rest of them will simply leave town. No one will ever know why, or give a damn. Everyone will be so deliriously happy that they're finally gone. It's just up to you to make certain they stay gone."

Frank chuckled and then continued, "There are those who thought that once I got into this position I would think only of myself. That I would take this power and use it selfishly. I am here to tell those people, and anyone else who thinks like them, that Junie Sando did not die in vain. There are some dues to be paid. They danced to the tune and don't expect to pay the piper, but they're going to pay. Oh, they're going to pay all right. They're going to pay sweetly, dearly and completely. They are going to pay so generously that they're going to curse their mothers for ever giving them birth. Danny Tiano, Jack Losse, Tuck Ryan, and precious Junie Sando, did not die in vain. If we allow their murders to go unavenged then we are inviting a curse on all our families, all our homes, and all our lives. What are we, if we are not people of substance? What are we, if we are not free? And we'll never, ever be free again, if we allow those dogs to laugh this off. They don't think we can do it. They don't think we have the nerve to do it. But you know what they think of us. They think we're just a bunch of small town, country hicks who can be pushed around, taken advantage of, and killed when it suits their fancy. Well, they're wrong. We are somebody! We are someone. We are invincible. We are Center Street." The Warriors jumped up and began to cheer. "We are Center Street!" Frank yelled and was echoed by the soldiers. "We are Center Street...!"

18

Teddy: "That is something that will continue to haunt me. And I'm aware, Joseph, I'll never be able to convince you or anyone else that I didn't relish the violence. I have always agreed with General Ulysses S. Grant who said, 'There was never a time when some way could not have been found to prevent the drawing of the sword.' And that's true, but Nick initiated it with us. We simply ran out of cheeks to turn."

Like a dismal fog creeping out of some brackish swamp that evening, a grim, windless hush fell over the city of Hudson. It was a tense, fragile silence, the kind that makes one want to talk fast, step lightly and peek around corners. Everyone seemed to be indoors, huddled in fear with their families. All sorts of persistent, frightening rumors were being bandied about. The Hudson City Police Station hadn't received so many telephone calls since VE Day in 1945.

Marty Politzsky's mouth was swollen and red where Frank Borzak had struck him. Ignoring it now, he was sitting in the Center Street office pleading with Janet Hammond, who was staring out into the night. "Janet, please listen to me. We can stop this before it's too late."

"It's already too late, Marty."

"There's been enough killing."

"Not on their side, there hasn't."

"Suppose they're waiting for our guys to come? Suppose they're waiting and kill some of them?"

"Our guys know what they're doing."

"Dear God, please help us," Marty moaned and grimaced.

"Why do you care about them?"

"I care. We all have to care about each other. Life must mean something to us all, or we'll lose it. We'll lose the meaning of it. Janet, what's happened to you?"

"Junie Sando is what's happened to me, Marty. Why hasn't he happened to you?"

"Junie would not allow this."

"Well, isn't that just terribly unfortunate. The one and only person who would have saved that bunch of pigs, they just happened to murder in cold blood."

Sighing, speaking softly, Marty said, "It wasn't supposed to be like this. It wasn't supposed to be like this at all. It was supposed to be...something good was to be accomplished. Not like this. Not like this at all. Not at all."

Spike Danner, Louis MacKey, and Burt Boone stepped from a green, '59 Ford into a black, silent, lifeless night. The back door of the Wentworth Hotel, which opened onto an alley, was wedged between two lines of garbage cans that stank from seven days of refuse. Three alley cats, having removed a few of the can tops, were feasting and barely glanced at the young intruders who were jimmying the lock on the door.

Once inside the basement hallway, which was straining to be lit by a single 30-watt light bulb, the three Streeters rode the freight elevator to the third floor. They knew the room number and the exact location in the building.

When a young woman came out of the room directly across the hall, Burt put his index finger to his lips. The woman, knowing who they were and the probable the reason they were there, simply nodded and rushed away.

Spike had his ear to the door. He could hear nothing. No movement. In a whisper, Louis suggested that perhaps Bummer Minghini was asleep. Pulling a snubnose .38 from his waistband, Spike indicated they were going in. Rushing into the room they found it vacated, the bed unmade, and the dresser drawers pulled out and empty. Burt ran to the bathroom and kicked open the door. No one was there.

In another part of the building, a window in a second floor room was being raised slowly. Simultaneously, as Skippy and Moe climbed into the room, the front door was flung open and Johnny Capp rushed in with his gun drawn. It took only seconds for them to realize they were too late.

Crying aloud, Johnny shouted, "Goddammit, we let 'em get away."

Just then, Kevin, Boris and Dominic came running down the hall. "Nappy's gone!" Kevin announced.

"We gotta go get 'em," Johnny shouted.

"Go get 'em!?" Kevin asked. "Where?"

When Spike, Louis and Burt rushed up to them, Johnny told them to get in their cars.

"For what?"

"What do you think, Burt? We' gotta' go after them, catch them!"

"We don't know where they are, or which way they went. We'll be on a wild goose chase."

"They're on their way to the City. They couldn't have left more than an hour ago. We'll get on the Parkway and catch 'em!"

"Johnny," Boris began calmly, "Hudson is our territory. We can't carry this war outside. We have no jurisdiction."

"Screw you and your jurisdiction! We can go where we want to and do what we want to. You know damn well we can't let Lido get away with what he did to Junie. Now get in the cars!"

When he shoved Dominic and Burt, Boris turned to Skippy and nodded toward Johnny. Grabbing Johnny, Skippy slammed him against the wall. Moe and Spike were holding his arms. Johnny was struggling and yelling for them to let him go. Gripping him around the throat and speaking softly, Skippy said, "It's over, Johnny. It's over. We've run them out of Hudson."

"So what!?"

Still struggling, Johnny began to cry. Boris stepped up, patted his cheek and said, "Don't worry, Lido will be staying up nights and looking over his shoulder for as long as one of us is alive. We'll make sure of it."

"That friggin' Frank!" Johnny whined. "If Teddy had been in charge of us we would have caught 'em. Frank screwed it up."

"Maybe we should thank Frank," Moe said.

"Thank him!?"

Moe smiled and said, "So far, we haven't done anything wrong. We're in the clear."

"Bullshit!" Johnny shouted bitterly. "We should have killed that son-of-a-bitch weeks ago!"

"Moe's right," said Boris. "We're all innocent. They can't arrest us for anything."

"They've got nothing on us," Kevin sighed in relief.

"Johnny, relax," Boris suggested. "We'll stop for now, but when the time is right, exactly right, we'll find a way to get to Lido. We'll get to him if it take years."

"Suppose he dies in the meantime?"

Dominic chuckled and said, "Then God will take care of him."

"Right," said Boris. "God will take care of it for us, and keep us all innocent."

When Skippy said, "Let's get out of here," Boris whispered to Moe, "I just hope Nick got out before Frank Borzak got to him."

Nick Coletti and his family gathered up all of their valuables and were quickly bringing the suitcases downstairs and placing them at the front door. Tony and Rosanna were dressed and waiting in the foyer as Sally came downstairs carrying an overnight bag.

"Make sure you got everything," Nick said. "We gotta get the hell out of here. I'll start taking some of this stuff out to the car."

Nick lifted two of the suitcases and rushed outside.

Opening the trunk to the black limousine, he dropped in one of the bags and heard, "Going somewhere, Nick?"

He turned just as Jeff, Butch, Stucko, and Frank approached him out of the dark. Frank snatched the car keys from Nick's hand.

"It's all over, Nicky baby," Frank said.

"You damn right it is! Haven't you heard?"

"Heard what?"

"The Governor. He's cleaning up the town tomorrow morning!"

"Cuff him," Frank ordered, and Jeff and Stucko did as they were told.

"Listen to me," Nick shouted. "I'm telling you the truth. There's going to be a thousand State Troopers and BCI men in here by the morning. They're going to arrest everybody in town."

"Bullshit."

"Frank, I'm telling you!"

"You're not telling me anything."

"I swear to you, Lido, Bummer and Nappy are already gone."

"They're gone all right."

"It's the truth. We would have been out of here by now except the kids took too much time getting ready. My men are gone."

"Yes, they sure are, right where you're going. To the claybanks."

"Frank, guys, I swear on my mother's grave!"

"Maybe he's telling the truth," said Butch.

"So what? They killed Junie."

"You know damn well I had nothing to do with that. Lido did it. I tried to stop him. I was satisfied with things the way they were between us."

"Tough shit, Nick."

Butch said, "Lido *is* the one who did it, Frank."

"I think Butch is right," Jeff added. "Why don't we find out if the State Troopers are coming?"

"It's got nothing to do with Junie!" Frank shouted.

"Frank, for God's sake, please!" Nick pleaded. "I've got a family. My children are waiting just inside the door. We're leaving Hudson for good."

Doubling Nick up with a knee to the groin, Frank shoved him into the trunk of the limousine and slammed it shut. Turning to Butch and Jeff, he said, "You two chicken livers can go hide your faces. Stucko and me will handle this."

"What if you find out in the morning he was telling the truth?" Jeff asked.

"It won't make a damn bit of difference to me. But if he's lying, it will make a big difference to you guys. You have my word on that. Let's go, Stucko!"

As Frank and Stucko got into the limousine and drove away, Butch and Jeff remained behind. And in the house, watching silently through a part in the drapes, little Tony Coletti had witnessed the entire incident.

19

Teddy: "What can I say, Joseph? Things happen."

The all-volunteer Hudson Fire Department consisted of three stations. Back then the men were mostly a noisy, slow-moving, destructive bunch of rowdies who were much more adept at getting drunk and raising hell than putting out fires. More than once, while attempting to bring a minor blaze under control, one of the adjoining wooden structures would go up in flames without their knowledge.

Janet Hammond was aware of the firemen's ineptness when she and Cindy Wells decided, with a few other Debs, not only to destroy all of the records of the organization, but the warehouse as well. At midnight, Junie Sando's and Jack Losse's bodies were secretly transferred to the Gilbert Funeral Parlor. Their families were to be notified the following morning.

Janet and the Debs scattered all the documentations, including names, ledgers, lists and financial statements, in the center of the hallway, doused them with gasoline, started the fire and then departed after nailing the doors shut. They had no concern that any of the information would ever be saved, or seen by anyone.

The alarm went out at 2 a.m. when the smoke was first seen billowing out of the warehouse. Ten minutes later the first truck, its station only four blocks away, arrived. The firemen rushed up to the doors, found them nailed, went back to the truck for their axes and then began to hack their way inside, only to be driven back by the holocaust which had already begun to engulf the building. It took the combined efforts of all three departments, six trucks and thirty-five men to get the blaze under control. By 6 a.m., the warehouse, which was completely gutted, had collapsed and was left a smoldering pile of ash.

The firemen were packing up their equipment when they heard the sirens off in the distance. Coming along Fairview Avenue, the thunderous rumbling shook the homes and awoke everyone in the neighborhood. Marty Politzsky, who lived in the suburban northeast section of Hudson, rushed out of bed and ran to the window. It was a long, constant line of black and white cars coming one after another filled with tall, stoned-faced men wearing sunglasses and big, gray, cowboy hats. They were armed and hell-bent for action. A little late perhaps, but they had arrived.

Realizing it was finally over, Marty sighed in relief. A bit sadly perhaps, but gratefully, definitely and permanently finished. Hurrying to get dressed, he rushed out of the house and caught a downtown bus as far as Fourth Street where the State Troopers had cordoned vehicles away from Diamond Street. Walking past the row of brothels, Marty could see that each house had been raided, but the Troopers were coming out empty-handed. Marty was joined by Janet Hammond as he crossed Third Street and, though neither said anything, they began to walk together. At the Apache Casino, the State Troopers had thrown all the gambling apparatus out into the parking lot. Several strong-armed officers were using sledge hammers to smash the slot machines and to break-up the blackjack and dice tables.

"I told you someone would listen," Mark Jansen said while coming up in back of Janet and Marty. "I just wish they would have listened sooner."

"How did you get them to come?" Marty asked.

"Fortunately, you young geniuses overlooked one extraordinary and super significant fact...this is an election year. The Governor is expecting a tough race. He didn't need this irritating thorn in his side."

"Did they catch anyone?" Janet asked.

"Not yet. Somehow word reached town during the night and all of them, the mayor, the chief of police, all the cops, the prostitutes, and Nick and his mangy crew escaped."

After a moment, Janet asked, "Mark...why didn't you go after them instead of us? Did that ever enter your mind?"

Mark was speechless.

But when Janet and Marty walked away, he called to them, "Hey, wait, there's a special agent from Albany who wants to talk to you guys."

"We aren't going anywhere," Marty assured him.

Butch Charles was standing off from the crowd. When he saw Janet and Marty, he joined them silently and they started toward Parade Hill Park.

It was a warm, cleansing, Hudson Valley day with a thousand fat-bellied clouds nearly blotting out the elusive sky. Here and there were strips and patches of luminous blue, and once in a while the inquisitive sun would peek through to glisten on the river.

Sitting on the lawn at the south end of the park were Teddy West and Augie Sando.

"I wonder when the State Troopers are gonna' come and git us," Augie ventured.

"Don't worry about it."

"I don't think I could stan' bein' in jail for very long. I hate small rooms and bein' all cooped up."

Teddy didn't answer this time.

"My fatha' went crazy when he heard the news about Junie," Augie said softly. "He started screamin' and everything. I neva' seen him like that before."

"I know. It's hard," said Teddy. "Someone once said that during peace-time, sons bury their fathers. But during wartime, fathers bury sons."

"My motha' went crazy, too," Augie continued. "They still don't understan' what happened even though I've told them a hundred times. The doctor had to come and give my fatha' somethin'. I had to git outta' there or I woulda' started cryin'...again."

Teddy took Augie's hand in his as Augie lowered his head. When Marty, Janet and Butch walked up to them, nothing was said as they all sat on the lawn.

A minute passed and they were approached by a stately, conservatively dressed man in a dark gray suit.

"I want to talk to you all for a moment."

The teenagers remained seated while the man took out his billfold. "My name is Agent Harold Pearson." He showed them his

F.B.I. identification. After looking at each of the teenagers carefully, he said, "Marty..."

They didn't expect the man to know any of their names.

"Teddy...Janet," Agent Pearson said and again looked at each one of them. "Don't ever try it again. Because if you do, I'll be here to stop you. Do you understand?"

Marty, Butch, Janet and Augie nodded.

"I mean it. You're all going to be watched very carefully from now on."

After Agent Pearson walked away, the group fell silent and remained so until Janet broke the silence with, "I saw old George Pugh kissing up to the State Troopers, directing them to certain houses. I'm sure he'll be in tight with them now."

Marty said, "My father says we're moving down to Poughkeepsie in a few days. He doesn't like it here anymore either."

While staring down at the grass and picking at a few blades, Butch said, "My father still thinks that Nick Coletti was a good man. A nice man to him anyway."

Janet looked at the boys and confessed, "My Mom came to my room for the first time in weeks late last night and we had a nice talk."

Teddy continued to pat Augie's hand while saying, "You know what we haven't done all summer?"

"What?" Butch asked.

"We haven't taken a ride on the ferry."

Without a word, all five teenagers got up and started toward the path that led down to the river and the boat docks.

"God, I'm gonna' miss Junie," Augie sighed.

"I think it's best we try not to think about that," Marty suggested.

"What should we do then?" Butch asked, sadly.

"Let's sing," Janet suggested in a vain attempt to put the thought of Junie's death aside. She began with, "*Gently sing the mocking birds as they're passing by...*"

When Janet was unable to continue, Teddy sang, "*Making up their different tunes while filling up the sky...*"

When Teddy couldn't go on, Butch began the chorus, "*Kee-ii, kee-oh...kee-ii, kee-oh, kee-ii...*"

Straining now and interspersed with tears and pain, they all joined in with, "*Kee-ii, kee-oh...kee-ii, kee-oh, kee-ii. Gently sing the mocking birds as they're passing by; making up their different tunes while filling up the sky...*"

Teddy: "They say you're only young once, but as we all know, once is enough if you live it right. If I had a second chance, I'd do it differently. I would want the same family, and to know Junie, of course, and Butch and Marty and some of my other friends. I would want to grow up in a small town like Hudson, but I would definitely change all the rest of it. Shortly after the Trooper raid, when Hudson returned to being a quiet, industrial town, a thirteen-year-old boy came up to me with tears in his eyes, spat in my face and said, `That's for losing it.' The generation after us and probably every generation in Hudson from then till now, feels as if they were cheated for having missed Center Street. Maybe they believe they could have handled it better; I don't know. But I would love to tell them that the pain and the everlasting grief and sorrow far outweighs any of the momentary joys of that summer."

Stunned by the revelations, Joseph Sherman was equally depressed. Assuming the interview was over, he leaned forward to stop the recorder. "Thank you, Mr. West. It's an incredible story. I'm sorry about Junie...and especially Tuck. If you don't mind me asking, what happened to the others?"

His face saddened, Teddy raised his head slowly, took a breath and said, "Augie is still in Hudson working in a lumber yard. Butch is a foreman at one of the ice plants. Frank, the last I heard, was a police officer out in Pittsburgh. Janet married some rich guy from California and they live in Marin County and have three children."

"Mary Granelli?" Joseph asked.

"She's one of those who simply disappeared."

Joseph took a moment before asking the next question. "Junie and Tuck are really dead, aren't they?"

"Yes."

"I think all of you are right. The story is too old and long gone to be of interest to anyone."

"Except you?"

Joseph nodded.

Removing the cassette from the recorder, Joseph stared at it for a moment while thinking *what a world* he had on that tape. After tossing it over to Teddy, he stood, moved to the door, turned and said, "My father was Tuck Ryan. My mother was pregnant with me when she left Hudson. A man named David Sherman fell in love with my Mom, married her and adopted my sister and me. My mother wouldn't tell me the story. I began to hear about it a little at a time. She finally broke it to me last year. She begged me not to follow it up."

"I'm sorry," Teddy said.

"You knew all along Tuck was my dad, didn't you?"

"Of course, we did."

"It killed him, Teddy. I never got to know him because he died for Center Street."

"You're right. And I have none of my usual mundane quotes to try and sheath it. He died and so did Junie and a lot of others. But Tuck *was* the most innocent of all."

"And I suppose you think that justifies it?"

"Nothing could ever justify what Lido Sandrelli did to Tuck Ryan."

"But you guys had the right to do what you did?" Shaking his head in disgust, Joseph continued, "You people really amaze me. Aren't you aware that Nick and all the rest were as innocent as Tuck when compared to the havoc you guys turned loose on Hudson? You used fear, threats, blackmail and extortion on your own people. And you ultimately committed cold, premeditated murder. And you were supposed to be the smart ones, intelligent, liberal, caring. You abused your power and literally destroyed a community, a culture. You were wrong! And you were evil."

Teddy reluctantly nodded in agreement. "Perhaps we should have handled it differently. My only defense is that we did what we had to under the circumstances. All of your Monday morning quarter-backing, Mr. Sports Quips and Quotes, can't alter the fact that *we* put an end to all that was really 'wrong' with Hudson. We did it. No one else."

"Yes, you did. But at what price? Do you want to know something? My mother's heart has never mended."

"Oh, Sherm. Sherm, aren't you aware that the line of broken hearts coming out of that period is endless? Endless."

"I seem to be a hell of a lot more aware of it than you are."

Teddy said, "If you would have been there, you would have joined right in and helped us. You would have been right in the thick of it."

Joseph shook his head while saying, "Never!"

When he opened the door to leave, Teddy said, "You forgot your coat." Moving over to the chair, he didn't lift Joseph's gray tweed, but instead took up the fur-lined trench coat and placed it around his shoulders. Grasping his forearm in the Center Street handshake, Teddy said, "We are..."

Joseph moved his shoulders so that the coat fell to the floor. He lifted his tweed and replied, "No, we're not," and walked into the hallway.

"Joseph."

He stopped, but wouldn't turn to face Teddy.

"There is one other thing that might interest you. It's suspected that some sort of retaliations are taking place. Boris Robanski, Stucko McNair, and Kevin Boone have been mysteriously killed. We're trying to figure out who's doing it. We want to make peace. Stop the violence. And do it nonviolently. We need someone to look into it. An investigator, a detective, or a hard-boiled reporter. Someone who knows how to dig. You wouldn't happen to know anyone like that, would you?"

"No, I wouldn't."

"We sure could use him. Someone who's not afraid of anybody or anything. Who's smart and can go out on his own and dig deep. Are you sure you don't know anyone like that?"

"No, I don't," Joseph said and continued down the hall to the elevator.

Low-hanging clouds began to creep around the mid-floors of Manhattan's tallest buildings, bringing with them the imminent threat of a storm. It was now 3:30 in the afternoon and the weather had turned even more bitter than it was in the morning. Joseph couldn't feel it. Back out on Fifth Avenue, he decided to walk for a while. Heading downtown, he was feeling the anguish as well as the relief of learning what had really happened to his father. Coming to a telephone, Joseph put a call into the *Herald*.

"Sherman, you all right?" were Beckman's first words.

"I'm fine. You and Mr.Henry were right. It was just a wild goose chase."

"Oh, well, kid, you're going to learn that for every good story there are ten of those. Come on back to the office. I've got an interesting bowling championship for you to cover and some Knick tickets for next week. And then we'll go out for some beers after work."

"All right," Joseph said and hung up.

Late that night, near 11:20 p.m., Joseph was sitting on his sofa. All the lights were out except for the blue-green fluorescent bulbs of the fish tanks. When the telephone rang, Joseph stared at it. On the fourth ring, he lifted the receiver.

"Yes?"

"Hi. This is Taylor."

"Taylor? I'm sorry, I don't think I know you."

"That's not very flattering."

"That's life. What can I do for you?"

"How do you know I'm not calling to do something for you?"

"Are you the dancer Sidney was telling me about?"

"Perhaps. What did he tell you?"

"Some nice things. Said you were scrumptious with legs and a body that could tear the heart out of a love-sick man."

"What else?" she asked.

"How much flattering do you need in one phone call?"

"I've heard some nice things about you, also."

"From Sidney?"

"Sidney, too. You're terribly handsome. You have a great body. You're extremely intelligent. You're single. Annnnd...you're a bona fide member of Center Street."

Joseph stopped breathing.

To break the silence, Taylor asked if she could come over. Joseph dropped the receiver back into the cradle. He lifted it and dialed Sidney. "What was that dancer's name?"

"The one you missed out on?"

"Was it Taylor?"

"Yes, Taylor. Taylor Morrant."

Joseph asked for her number, got it and called.

"What took you so long?" she asked.

"I'm slow. Do you still want to come over?"

"What do you have in mind?"

"The same thing you do."

"Not now, you don't."

"I'm not a member of Center Street."

"Okay," Taylor said simply.

"Who said I was?"

"Come on, you know. They need you. Members are being elimi-nated. We're trying to keep it quiet, just between a few of us. There are certain unsavory characters who, if and when they find out, would take advantage of this situation to get things started again. We want to make peace as quickly and easily as possible. You know you're going to do it."

"Are you a member?" Joseph asked.

"Would you like it if I were?"

"Maybe."

"Would you love it if I were?"

"Perhaps."

"I'm coming over," she said.

"Forget it."

"You're not going to be able to resist, Joseph. Me, your mission, or...Center Street."

the end

NEXT: *Part Two of the Trilogy.*

CENTER STREET
II
"The Second Generation"
The Women